Thirty

Blinding White

Flashes

A Collective of Short Stories

by

Erik R. Eide

Table of Contents

Preface

A collection of short stories seemed like an easy plan for a book. I have always enjoyed writing shorts. They have emerged at random times without my foreknowledge. The small book you are now reading was planned but unexpectedly challenging to write as the busyness of life encroached upon my writing time.

For this collection, I chose a theme inspired by the quasi-science fiction narrative used in the old black and white show from the late fifties/early sixties- "The Twilight Zone." I loved how that television series had a way of causing you to contemplate its stories beyond themselves. These tales sometimes affect you in profound ways running deeper than the show's theme itself. By today's standards, its special effects are hokey, enforcing the need for us to rely on our imagination to pull out the screenplay writer's focus. The subject matter always varied, yet the common thread with every show was how the writers tried to present reality from a different angle. I wanted to emulate those shows in my way. Some of these adventures are meant to provoke more profound thoughts in your own experience. There are serious dramas, others whimsical. Hopefully, all will entertain.

This small book could be a perfect companion for an airline flight. You might just want to skip the first story and read it after you arrive at your destination. Once again, thank you for being on the other side of my writing. It gives me a feeling of thirty blinding white flashes!

-Erik

The Flight

"Would you mind if I took the aisle seat? That is if you don't mind the window. I don't mind the window but, I would appreciate the aisle seat if it became necessary. You see, I had a very large breakfast...."

The man in the light green polo shirt rambled on as Pricilla attempted to jam her carry-on into the already overstuffed bin.

He continued, "Really, I should manage if you prefer the aisle. I know when I was a child, the aisle seat...."

Pricilla's patience with her seat neighbor and the stress associated with the task at hand were wearing thin. The bag would not fit. By no means weak, she was an athletic woman, and she wasn't worried about damaging anything in her luggage. She gave up on the location and resolved to sit down, bag on lap, until the crowd died down. The teenage boy behind her leaned over, saying,

"Ma'am, I can put that down there if ya'll like.", he pointed to the last overhead on the right.

"Thank you so much!" relinquishing the bag to the abnormally polite young man, she turned her attention to the man in the light green polo. He was still rambling on as she caught back up with him.

"... that's the main reason for my difficulty with earrings.", he smiled a confidently dis-attached smile. In the flash of time it took to analyze him, she settled on the sense that he was harmlessly missing a screw or two.

"No, that's fine. I don't mind the window." Pricilla glanced back at the teenager to find his tall, gangly frame lifting the awkward bag and jamming it ferociously into the bin. He must have seen me trying earlier, she thought, amused with his actions. She then wearily stood up to allow Green Polo to exit the seats. Settling in at the window, she buckled in as the intercom came alive with the voice of a calm professional.

"Good afternoon, this is your Captain Peter Stolp. I hope you enjoyed your stay in New York City. We should have good headwinds into O'Hare today, giving us a revised arrival at about 3:25 this evening. Blue skies and about 85 degrees should greet you on arrival to Chicago. The flight attendants will be down the aisle after take-off. Thank you for choosing Time Airlines, and we hope you enjoy your flight."

The flight attendants performed their safety dance with a belt, buckle, and inflatable vest props. The two near the front of the plane looking bored, knowing the passengers were equally unimpressed. The third attendant nearest Pricilla and Green Polo attempting to liven it up with goofy body language and knowing smiles to the passengers. She accidentally pulled the vest's inflation cord too sharply, and it inflated with a loud bang. Passengers with their backs to her spun around in shock while those of her audience erupted with laughter and handclaps at the surprise. The poor young lady was shocked that her prop had been substituted with a "live" vest, rolled with it, and did a little curtsy before walked to the rear of the plane to remove the offensive article. Her admirers continued to cheer as she retreated.

Pricilla leaned into the wall against her pillow as the Airbus A330 left the runway. The familiar mechanical dog barking sounds within the plane somewhere subsided as the landing gear retracted. Green Polo continued his monologue to a young man in a business suit who had sat down just before the safety floorshow. Gray Suit also gave up on responses to Green Polo as he, too, leaned his seat back and drifted into oblivion after a frantic week of meetings deep within Manhattan's financial towers. Green Polo shrugged his shoulders and pulled the safety card out of the pocket in front of him. In fact, the entire plane, with the exception of the flight crew, slowly fell into a deep sleep as the jet leveled off gently. The de-vested flight attendant began her backward stroll down the aisle to the front of the coach. Noticing the entire plane was out cold, she looked at her co-worker James, who was pushing the cart of beverages and pretzels, saying,

"They're all out! I've never seen this before. Weird."

"Well, I guess we can put the cart back. I'm not waking um up for soda and pretzels.", James replied, looking like a used napkin, feeling less surprised by the passengers' nap and more desiring to join them. He had been awake for close to 24 hours after flight delays and a scheduling mistake by Time Airlines. The two of them moved the cart back to the rear of the plane. James found three seats against the rear bulkhead empty, calling his name.

"I'm gonna take a quick nap, Karen. Wake me up if they do-okay. Better yet, sit down a while. They're not going anywhere."

"I want to check on Sarah first.", smiled Karen. After thousands of flights, she was feeling just a bit strange about this one. Once again, she made her way to the front of the cabin, noting everyone seated except for Green Polo was out cold. She found Sarah sitting in the jump seat of the bulkhead looking a bit confused. This Flight was Sarah's first as lead, and she had enough imagination to think she was being pranked.

"This isn't funny. It's weird!" Sarah exclaimed, nails flashing with her hand gestures, "How did you guys pull this one off?" Karen and James often targeted Sarah for practical jokes but never while working.

"I wish this was our work Hun but, it isn't. I'm a little freaked out. Was that you with the vest swap!" eying Sarah in mock anger.

"Nope, wasn't me, not worth my job, Honey. That was weird, though. Must've been the clean-up crew? I dunno but, what's with all of these people? It's not like it's 1 AM. I already let Dave know. He said just to take it easy."

"Okay, well, you're the boss! Then I'm going to sit down too. I'm wiped." Karen walked back down the aisle seeing every face either snoring or with a trail of drool from each smile. Passing Green Polo, she found him asleep as well. His loud snores seemed to equal his voracity for communication. James was leaning against the wall and snoring as well when she made it to the back of the plane. For some reason, seeing James out caused panic to arise within her. She quickly walked back to Sarah, finding her in the same state. She picked up the intercom to the cockpit.

"Peter, this is getting even weirder. Both James and Sarah are out cold.", no response, dead air. "Peter, are you there? Vijay, are you there?", no answer from the co-pilot, just the white noise of the aircraft's gentle flight came through the receiver. Karen was terrified. She walked back to Sarah and tapped her shoulder, then shook it. The only response was a gentle coo like a newborn. Making her way through the cabin with failed attempts to wake passengers, she gave up and sat on the ground halfway down coach. Sobbing, she sent up a prayer,

"Dear God, I know I haven't spoken with you in a while. Please protect me. I'm so scared." She decided it was best to stay alert and made her way to the cockpit door. She entered the security code within the panel inside the locker to the right of the cockpit. The lock opened with a loud click, and she stepped inside. Both Captain Peter Stolp and Co-pilot Vijay Saha were in a deep sleep, the plane in autopilot mode. Karen pulled the headset off Vijay's head and pulled out the connector, plugging into the jack nearest her.

"O'Hare, this is flight 835 out of JFK. Do you copy?" dead air, no response. She repeated her call two more times and gave up. She began to descend into deep despair. Tremors shook her in waves of panic as her heart raced. Leaving the Captain and Co-pilot to their dreams, she somehow managed to lock the cockpit door. Fearing this to be a terror plot or one of a handful of parallel theories running through her mind, she double-checked the lock to ensure it was secure. The walk back to the rear of the plane became clouded through her eyes as she collapsed on the floor, halfway through first class. Karen

4

amazed herself as she regained conciseness and was slightly miffed she couldn't just stay out. She thought better of staying incoherent and made her way to the galley to brew a pot of coffee.

The hours passed by slowly as Karen drank pots of coffee, too unnerved to consider falling asleep. Eight more hours passed as the terror lingered on for her. The plane was somewhere over the Pacific Ocean. She continued to pray and felt that she should eat. The passenger feed, as she referred to it in her mind, surprisingly, satisfied and comforted. After another hour, the coffee couldn't hold off her exhaustion as she slumped down next to James in the back row. She immediately fell into a deep sleep.

At once, there were thirty blinding white flashes outside the aircraft, then calm. The captain woke and gently shook Vijay. They resumed their duties, unaware of anything abnormal presently. James and Sarah yawned and stretched respectively at either end of the cabin as all the passengers came alive within their seats. Karen was OUT. James attempted to wake her to no avail, giving in and placing a blanket over her. The captain turned to Vijay,

"I dunno what happened, but we've overshot Chicago. We're off the coast of Oregon! I don't understand. The log shows we've been in the air for over ten hours! Even that doesn't make sense. We're about to run out of fuel!"

"What The Hell! Peter, I don't remember even falling asleep. I just leaned back and stretched a minute ago! Are you sure?

"I know, I thought the same thing! This is weird. Look at the clock! Maybe Control has something. PDX, this is flight 835 out of JFK. We're off course and disoriented.", dead air. Captain Stolp repeated his hail to Portland International several times. Switching to the civilian emergency channel "GUARD," on the VHF radio at 121.5 MHz, he began his hail again, "GUARD, this is Flight 835 out of JFK, do you copy?" the familiar static was the only reply. "GUARD, we are changing course to PDX. Please have an emergency on stand-by."

Captain Stolp banked sharply back toward Portland and began the descent. Addressing the cabin,

"Good evening folks, we've experienced some issues beyond our control and will be landing in Portland International shortly. Please raise your tray tables and seats to the upright position. We should be on the ground soon."

The plane dropped closer to the ground as the water below came into focus. Mount Hood towered in the distance ahead as The Captain pointed to a large field below to Vijay.

"We're not going to make it to PDX. I think we should have plenty of room there.", He was glad for the fact that it was early afternoon with good visibility. He had never landed an emergency before in reality as he leaned into the countless hours of flight simulator training.

Thirty blinding white flashes outside the plane overpowered sight just before Pricilla rubbed her eyes while waking. She looked around her to find everyone asleep, including the flight attendants. Looking out the window, she could see lights far below in the darkness, like stars, emanating from the small towns of the farmlands in the distance. Inside the cockpit, the captain and co-pilot continued their dreams. The passengers, unaware, continued their blissful dream state. Pricilla rose from her seat to use the restroom. Upon exiting, she noticed both flight attendants asleep in the back row of seats. Thinking this was odd, she went to the front of the plane to speak with the attendant in first class. While walking to the front of the aircraft, reality began to sink in as she became fully awake. Everyone was asleep. The first-class attendant, out cold. Pricilla pounded on the cockpit door to no avail. There was no sense in fighting it; she decided to take a first-class seat. Her mind raced. It didn't make sense, and it was dark outside. They should've landed by now, no one was there to answer her questions, and she was rational enough to let the irrational define itself apart from her experience. She decided to have a glass of champagne and a first-class meal while she waited. The airline owed her as much. She ate a nice dinner and had several glasses of champagne before falling back asleep.

Once again, thirty blinding white flashes strobed outside the jet as it cruised at thirty thousand feet. The freshly plowed and leveled field came up fast after the captain retracted the landing gear for a belly landing. His voice came over the intercom within the cabin.

"Prepare for impact!", Most passengers realized what was happening, the rapid descent followed by the sound of the engines reducing power one by one. The plane, eerily quiet as it glided toward the Oregonian soil below. It may have been the rest given prior to the landing, or possibly it was this group of people but, everyone was calm, to those that thought about it, that in and of itself was odd. The plane leveled off for what seemed to be a much longer time than what would be expected on a landing strip. The passengers watched fields flash by on either side of the plane. Herds of cows, power poles, roads, and barns flashed by like subliminal messages. Then, moving a bit closer still, grain as a blur, it's ripe gold-tone pattern-less to color all around.

Further lower to their correct perception as the landing gear was stowed, they sped, gliding feet above the field that changed from gold to a rich black smooth perfection. The plane slowly began to touch soil. At first, the sound was similar to turbulence, gradually becoming more violent as the captain engaged the spoilers and reversed thrust as he would have on any landing strip. It was either Captain Stolp's skillful long approach, the extended field length, the excellent soil of Oregon, or the diligence of a conscientious farmer that provided a landing similar to that of an actual airstrip. The plane once again became a body at rest after expending its energy against the rich black earth. The passenger compartment filled with relieved occupants echoed with sighs and cheers of relief.

Immediately the occupants returned to their original form. All stood, filling the aisle, as though late for a meeting. They gently pushed past each other to retrieve belongings from the overheads. Older or weaker passengers succumbed to the animal tendencies of those aloof of their surroundings and its occupants.

Thirty blinding white flashes occurred yet again as Karen woke to the commotion around her. The plane was on the ground, to her relief. She looked toward the front of the cabin, amazed at the sight of everyone awake again. It didn't matter that she once again was witnessing some of the society's less admirable attributes. She was no longer within a nightmare. Captain Stolp and Co-Pilot Saha opened the cockpit door to cheers from the entire plane. Amazingly there were no injuries, except for a few people needing oxygen after their panic attacks. The exit doors were opened, slides deployed, and passengers made their way off the plane. Many kissed the loamy black soil as soon as they could. Once everyone had disembarked, the flight crew made its way down the slides.

The passengers slowly separated out into subsets. Those possessing leadership traits decided to send a group to the nearest farmhouse to contact the authorities. Pricilla, Karen, Vijay, and Grey Suit were chosen to go. The captain chose a few more people to keep the survivors together. They then began to pull luggage from the holds in case their wait was an extended one.

The appendage group began its amoeba stretch toward the farmhouse, a good mile away from the center of the vast black field. Stepping through the tilled soil was similar to walking through fresh snow, without the frozen toes to make the journey toilsome. There was a point in the short hike when everyone stopped and, with an unknown connection, gazed into one another's eyes and just wept. They were tears of relief, joy, and the realization and appreciation of the fundamentals of life. After no more than a minute, the four stopped, visibly shaken, smiled at each other with a knowing depth. No words were spoken. None were needed. They all turned back to the task at hand, each newly bonded to these three strangers.

Eventually, they reached the farmhouse. Calling out, Vijay found no response. They walked the grounds to find nobody anywhere. All outbuildings were without reply. It seemed the only resident was a lonely yellow Labrador Retriever who made his way to the group from one of the outbuildings. Looking relieved to see them, he eventually led them to his food bowl. Picking up the bowl in his mouth, dropping it in front of the plastic garbage can labeled "Thor." Karen opened the can and filled up Thor's bowl with dog food. The dog emptied the bowl in less than two minutes as his tail became a blur.

"Well, you're a hungry boy, aren't cha!" Karen said in her best doggy-loving voice. Thor's entire body became as excited as his tail once was. He practically knocked her over with joy as she scratched his back. "Well, Thor, where are your people?" Amazingly, Thor slowly walked off then, turned back several times until the group followed. He led them to the shop. There was an old combine filling most of the building. The rear was up on jacks, one wheel on the ground, a partial bearing job completed. The dog walked over to the wheel next to a shop seat with a tray underneath filled with tools. Thor stood next to the chair and began to bark. The empty seat did nothing. The dog continued to bark as the seat sat there alone in silence, as the group started to feel disturbed.

Gray Suit spoke first, "I'm not sure what's wrong with the dog but, we need to keep moving if nobody's home here.

"Yeah, this is kinda creepy anyway, um.. ya know I don't know your name. I'm Pricilla." Gray Suit smiled and turned toward Pricilla, saying,

"I'm Nathaniel," he paused and said," sorry, call me Nate.", addressing the group, "Maybe we can take the car in the driveway into the nearest town. My cell's still useless. Anyone got a signal?", All shook their heads, Vijay responded,

"Hopefully, we can see a sign once we get on the road."

"Sounds good," Nate replied as all agreed. They made their way to the 64'Lincoln in the driveway, finding the keys still in the ignition. The classic piece of art history waited there as though needing to be driven. Vijay opened the driver's door as it made the familiar groan of a car of that era. Pricilla took shotgun at the same time the two rear suicide doors were opened by Nate and Karen. The two backward-opening rear doors and front passenger door groaned in harmony while in motion. Four heavy doors closed in rapid progression gave an uncanny satisfying feeling by their sounds. Vijay reached for the keys as the old engine slowly turned with reluctance then roared to life. The pale green Continental backed out to the empty roadway and headed east toward Portland on highway 26.

"Any idea where we are?" asked Pricilla while pulling down the visor to check her makeup, "Looks desolate."

"The last sign said highway 26. We've gotta be northwest of Portland. Any further west, and we'd be in foothills. I took 26 about ten years ago out to Cannon Beach from Portland. We're in the farmlands near the city, I'd say about forty minutes away or so.", said Nate looking at Pricilla in the mirror. Just then, a sign read, "8 Mi. North Plains exit 57". Farmlands passed by them as they floated along the highway, continually reminded of their gift of life. Exit 57 came into view as Vijay instinctively put on his turn signal though they hadn't seen anyone on or off the road thus far. The car turned onto Glencoe Road and crossed over the highway north toward North Plains. They pulled into a gas station, finding it deserted yet, there were signs of recent activity everywhere. Empty cars and trucks, new and old, sat at the pumps and in the parking spaces. A pile of packaged food lay on the counter near the register. Dried-out hotdogs rotated on their ferris wheel; the heat lamp relentlessly oblivious to their dehydration continued its torture. The bathroom key was still inserted in the lock of the women's room, waiting to be returned to the front desk.

"This is weird, but I gotta use the ladies' room!" Karen bolted toward the restroom, finding the key in place to her relief. Upon returning to the group, they decided to try the station across the street. The other side of the road yielded similar results from the cars out front to the hotdogs' plight, this time upon a sort of heated dynamometer, the output results much better than the Ferris wheel across the street. There was no one in sight. The uneasiness was palpable as Nate suggested a trek deeper into town. As the Lincoln rolled down Glencoe Road, they witnessed a seemingly recent ghost town. Stores, homes, warehouses, and government buildings, vacant, only lonely pets wandered the streets, ducking out from behind houses as they heard the car pass by.

"Can we go? I think we should leave. Something must've happened here, and Portland's not far. It might be dangerous to linger.", Karen pleaded as everyone agreed both logically and emotionally. After Vijay reset the pump at the register, they filled up the car and headed back toward Portland on highway 26. The closer they came to the city, they found vehicles that had been pulled off the road as though knowing the way would need to be cleared for them. There were what seemed to be traffic jam quantities of vehicles on either side of the wide-open road. The city gradually came into view. They saw pets filling the streets before and behind them, close to fifty in all. Arriving in the city center, after the traffic jam of pets had slowed their travel, they exited the car. The dogs and cats looking confused and relieved to see them, drew near.

It became clear to all; Portland and the surrounding areas were abandoned. There was no sign of human contact, only memories of its remnants. The small group began to feel the truth in their bones. The pets drew closer, longing for their touch. It was a surreal petting zoo. In retrospect, they were grateful for the press of the animals upon them. It actually took some of the edge off of the situation.

"I think we're done here; we should get back before dark," said Pricilla, who was beginning to feel exhausted with emotions.

"Yeah, but I think we need to bring some supplies back with us. I don't think the Lincoln's gonna have enough room. We should look for a truck." Nate replied, being careful to be sensitive to the group.

"I saw a pickup about a block back that way. I'll go see if it's got keys." Vijay responded.

"We need to find food, medical supplies, camping supplies might not be a bad thing either. This is gonna freak a lot of people out. We might be camping back at the field for a while." added Karen. The group fanned out within a couple of blocks finding everything needed to fill the pickup within an hour and a half. They managed to tear themselves away from the dogs and cats after raiding a pet store and feeding them all before heading back to the crash site.

The trip back was silent for the first half. It was then decided that Vijay would inform the captain first. The farmhouse came into view along with most of the survivors wandering or huddled in groups nearby it. Vijay brought the pickup to a stop at the end of the driveway as Captain Peter strolled up to meet them.

"What's all this stuff for, Vijay?"

"Pete, we need to talk." The group exited the crew cab and began unloading, glad they didn't have Vijay's task. Peter Stolp and Vijay Saha had been co-workers for many years, and the captain knew when Vijay was joking. He was a terrible liar. Peter could spot his lightly quivering left eyebrow easily when he was teasing. He had secretly longed to play poker with Vijay one day but avoided his worst intentions. Vijay's eyebrows were solid as he spoke concisely, narrating their entire trip like a flight plan. Peter saw everything through Vijay's words, and terror filled his heart. Thoughts of his wife and kids, friends, and extended family were mixed with confusion and wonder. He believed his friend but wanted to

12

believe he was mistaken. There was too much to do tonight. His first obligation was to the passengers and his crew.

"I tried to call Vi earlier. Phones are working but, I couldn't get any answers, not even 911. I don't want to believe you, Vijay. We've got to try again tomorrow. Maybe Seattle is different. Tonight, we've got to keep things quiet about this if we can. Let's focus on getting people settled."

"Okay, Pete, I don't think we have any other choice. It's getting late." As they were finishing their settlement that night, pets from nearby towns filed into the camp. The survivors, most of which grateful for their presence, welcomed them in out of the elements.

The following day Peter and three others made a trip to Seattle. They arrived late that night with a moving truck filled with food, supplies, and pet food. They also brought the news of a similar fate encountered in that northwestern city. The entire journey there and back was met with the same strange post-apocalyptic sights. Peter, Vijay, Karen, and Nate, together with a few more survivors, formed a leadership team to prepare for the future. They still had no idea what had happened to the west coast and decided to head east to see if things were different there after winter.

Autumn and winter passed as the survivors fanned out to the neighboring farms and town. Most had come to realize this was their new life, many still mourning the loss of family, friends, and the recent memory of earth's society. Others eager to start afresh while, holding memory within their hearts, pressed on with life. Many were taught various professions by each other. Doctors, farmers, mechanics, among others, taught those left without a place in this new world. There was no need for stockbrokers, computer technicians, nuclear physicists, and the like at this point in their small community.

"This is Elsa Thomsen with a WGN special report. The NTSB search for Time Airlines flight 835 has been called off after a year without revealing its whereabouts. The airline's

CEO Morgan Roberts has made a formal statement.", the camera feed changed to the view of a graying man in his early sixties behind a Time Airlines podium.

"It is with my deepest regrets and sympathies to the friends and families of the passengers and crew of Time Airline's flight 835 that I must now concede to the loss of the aircraft and its occupants. The NTSB and other federal, state, and international organizations have failed to find any trace of the airliner. Our prayers are forever with them, their friends, and families." The world carried on except for those closely impacted by the loss of loved ones. To most, it was merely another drop of sand through the hourglass of time.

In the farming community outside of Portland, the survivors settled into their new lives. Most were thankful for it, the crash survival, and a reset to life in general. There were no credit card debts, mortgages, or any other outstanding responsibilities to weigh them down. There were more than enough supplies in the cities to draw on.

After ten years or so, the remaining survivors met at the annual crash site memorial. They took their places in their assigned seats and were served a much more enjoyable meal than any airline of this era would provide. There were Champagne toasts, speeches, and memories shared, laughter and tears mingled throughout. After the dinner, the removal of its trays and trash. The group customarily bowed their heads in remembrance and prayer over the loss of their previous life. As the last passengers lowered their heads, thirty blinding white flashes strobed outside the crash site.

Pricilla was woken to a familiar voice,

"Looks like my need for the aisle has kicked in, ma'am!" Green Polo said as he unbuckled and rose to his feet in a panic. "That was a strange dream.", she thought to herself as she looked around the cabin, finding many passengers also waking from sleep. She turned to look out the window at thirty thousand feet just as there were thirty blinding white flashes outside   the   plane.

The Field

I was still waking up, even after my second cup of coffee. The thermos was almost empty. Desperation was setting in. Yesterday was a wrecking ball to all of my plans; work was piling up with no end in sight. Though previously started jobs awaiting parts began to mold in my clipboard, the service calls kept coming in. The last thing I wanted this morning was to start my day with an early call to Moreco, and to be an omniscient narrator to this story, I had enough work. The receiving door's lock buzzed as I grabbed the handle. I could never remember whether or not to turn it or just pull. Every customer was different. My torque met with immovable resistance then, I pulled. Why the heck am I telling you this? I have no clue. I guess its got something to do with my new narration job. I really don't have the time to screw with this today! I've got customers waiting, for god's sake! Clair was behind the counter, Emma at the desk behind her, grinding out received data back to Moreco's corporate offices.

"Hey, Chris! You look like death!" teased Clair as I walked in. The receiving department employees at Moreco had that air of superiority when it came to being alert at 6AM. They should brag; it was practically lunchtime for them. Doug was at the dock as I yelled,

"Hey, Doug, what's wrong this time?"

"Morning, Chris, you look pretty crappy!"

"Thanks, Doug!"

"Travel's been cutting out all morning." He reached for the double jacks yoke and twisted the grip as I watched along with Clair and Jake- the receiving forklift operator who had stopped offloading to join in the conversation, saying,

15

"Bob's been bitchin' all morning, "F-ing thing's (look, I know I have to be the narrator for this thing but, I'm not going to swear while telling it okay. Look, I know I'm far from perfect but, I don't talk like that so, you'll just have to use your imagination to fill in the blanks if you want to fill your head with that crap. Look, I said I wasn't perfect, okay! I just think a lot of the people I work around could find a few more adjectives for their vocabulary and stuff. Sorry to interrupt Jake..) "only a few weeks old!"

"Yep, that's what a warranty's for." I think it's kinda funny people expect something new not to break down or need adjustments. They are, after all, built by people, not gods. My wife used to think that way until she realized some of my work involved removing the gremlins from new machines under warranty. Back to the dock, Doug was still moving the grip back and forth as the large power jack slowly rolled back and forth each way a few inches flawlessly. Just then, out of the corner of my eye, I caught a glimpse of a small object that darted beneath the forks of the machine as it silently rolled. Clair saw it too and yelled to Doug.

"Stop! There's something under the jack!" The small dark brown shape darted out, then back under the truck near the drive tire. Imperceptibly to all but myself- I am the narrator, ya know, Doug got a devious look in his eyes as he slowly turned the grip forward, the jack moving no more than an inch. There was a subdued pop like that of a fresh ping-pong ball popping as the tire rolled over the head of the vole. He instantly felt ashamed as everyone involved had been silent just before the pop that sounded like a firecracker to them.

"Really, Doug? That's cruel and disgusting." Clair turned and went back to work checking in orders. Everyone else did the same as Doug shrugged with a weak smile, handing over the controls.

I brought the jack outside and completed the repair. The problem was associated with an interlock switch. On a microscopic level, one electron left the battery's positive pole, ran through one of the fine wires of the twisted braid of the power cable inside its insulation. It went through the 15 amp control fuse, made it past the closed key switch then, stopped dead at the common side of the brake interlock switch. The wire itself was broken clean off due to the movement of the handle's pivot and an assembler's misjudgment in wire routing. The first electron, we'll call him Duane, was highly annoyed. He was known for having a foul mouth but, we've already discussed the language I'm accustomed to. Duane stood still, anticipating that in a nano-second, trillions of his co-workers would be there, being pushed by the voltage all of them were tormented by. All he wanted to do was get past this damned switch, through the logic controller, and back to the negative battery terminal where he could rest awhile. The nano-seconds piled up for an eternity as I diagnosed the issue with the control circuit of the jack. I made the repair to the wiring and rerouted it to prevent future problems for Duane and his friends. By the way, Duane did make it back to the negative pole of the battery, unless, of course, you prefer negative flow electron theory, whereas he would have made it back safely to the positive pole. The differing opinions of electrical engineers and their theories never have impressed me much. In my mind, look, I know I'm just a tech, not a scientist but, it doesn't matter much in the real world which way an electron flows as long as I can see its path on my schematic. I don't think the electron cares either. You'll have to ask Duane if you really care.

Doug walked out the door and strolled up to me while lighting a cigarette. I guess smokers don't think you mind their smoke as long as you're outside and a blue-collar type guy. I didn't really care. Doug was a longtime customer of fifteen or so years. He liked to small talk on his smoke break when I showed up. Just then, I saw a tiny flash of brown under the jack again. Before I could comment, there were thirty blinding white flashes all around us, and Doug was GONE! His cigarette dropped out of the same area occupying his hand previously. I looked around, stunned; well, I guess that version of myself did. The parallel universe narrator side of me knew exactly what was happening while the real-world me wondered if someone slipped something into my last cup of coffee. The real world me just stared at Doug's cigarette for a minute and ran to the receiving door to get help.

Doug appeared to have vanished. In reality, he had become Micro-Doug and was now surrounded by ten voles underneath the jack. One vole powerfully addressed Doug, now far superior in size and tone to the micro-receiving manager.

"You are charged with the murder of Voltaire! Everything you say and do can be used against you. If you hold back any information, this will hinder your defense. Cuff him, Volly!" A large black vole pulled a set of handcuffs from his belt and secured Doug, who was so stunned, he wondered what he had been smoking earlier. Volly picked him up and set him on the back of another vole as the group scurried away from under the jack toward the retention pond and its surrounding flora. The trial was quick, precise, and airtight. Doug was rightfully convicted of vehicular homicide in the first degree and sentenced to death by crushing the following morning. Volly lead him back to his cell, an upside-down paper cup with a hole chewed through it for access. The large vole led him to his cell and said,

"Sorry Doug, you don't seem like the murdering type. Did you know what you were doing?"

"Ya know Volly, I had no idea voles were as sophisticated as they are. I guess as long as something looked insignificant to me, it wasn't worth a thought. "I didn't kill Voltaire with the knowledge of his intellect or any real value. In my eyes, he was just a field mouse! My thinking has changed dramatically in the last few hours." Volly sat on his haunches listening to Doug's words. Unimpressed and dissuaded by Doug's pleas, he simply plugged the hole in the cup with a large peanut and scurried away.

In the middle of the night, Doug was awakened by the sound of something sniffing around the outside of the cup. He lay there on the turf, fearing what would happen next. There was a thump on the ground as he heard a ruckus in the den near the cup. The voles were in turmoil, rushing to exit the area as a lone coyote pinned down and quickly consumed two of the community's finest politicians (from their point of view, that is.) It, the coyote, just happened to bump into the cup, knocking it over. Once the beast caught the scent of a human, not knowing this was only Micro-Doug, it ran for its life, like most coyotes do from humans. Doug had his undeserved reprieve. He quickly, though, not scurry speed, left the retention pond finding a child's toy nearby for cover. It was an old forgotten steel dump truck. Doug could have driven it if it actually had an engine, controls, and brakes. This one wasn't equipped as such but, the cab was a perfect shelter. He found a somewhat clean old rag nearby and pulled it to the truck making his nest complete. Exhausted, he settled in for the night, to what, to his surprise, was a very comfortable night's sleep. Maybe it was his size or the accouterments about him as he woke up hours before sunrise feeling completely rested. It was the voices nearby that roused him from slumber. He recognized one from yesterday; the other was unfamiliar.

"Look, I know it's dangerous. That's half the challenge!"

"I just think you're a bit young for that kinda challenge, Cletus!" said Volly to his teenage vole.

"I'll be careful, Dad, I promise."

"Be back for breakfast, and don't do anything stupid."

"Thanks, Dad, I will. You'll see!"

The sleeker and younger of the two voles scurried away as Volly watched, feeling conflicted, knowing his son was almost grown and he would have to give in to his son's instincts sooner or later. It was easier when his wife was alive. They could share the load when it came to the changes, good or bad, their fifty offspring brought to their lives. The draw to 'The Field' was difficult for him to watch his oldest transition to. It was a time-honored position all voles were assigned to, no need for a draft. This was their reason for existence.

Doug's eavesdropping had piqued his interest beyond curiosity. There was an intensity burning within him to see what kind of danger they were talking about. He stopped for a minute while watching Volly's son move below the truck, picking up supplies from under a nearby tuna can. He thought,

"Why are you so interested, Doug? Go back to bed. Figure out this thing in the morning. These are mice, for god's sake!" Ignoring the voice of reason within him, he carefully climbed out of the truck and followed Volly's son.

He stayed a safe distance from the young vole to stay undetected as he watched him leave the safety of the retention pond to cross the parking lot between it and the Moreco. The young vole came to the rollup door at the receiving department and found his entry point, a small air gap between the door and the building. Doug was amazed while watching his quarry move past the opening with ease. He, too, entered the building just in time to watch the vole move to the power-jack associated with yesterday's events. The vole moved into the guts of the machine and hesitated for a second as Doug moved out of sight below. Feeling safe, Doug pressed on, surprising himself to find that climbing up and through the jack took much less effort than he has suspected. He arrived just in time to watch the young creature with yesterday's repaired wiring in his vole hands. The wire was handled with the precision of a surgeon as the vole opened his mouth, placing it between two razor-sharp teeth. The action was delicate, methodical, and precise as the wire was snipped in half effortlessly. The vole then took each half of the wire, setting the ends as close together as possible. It backed away from its work as one wire fell away slightly. He grabbed both ends again, manipulating them until satisfied. Once again, he stood back away from his work for the inspection. The two wire halves now appeared as one, his fieldwork complete. The vole turned to leave and was surprised to find Doug in his path as he stopped in his tracks.

"Why did you do that?" Doug questioned.

"Do what? I didn't do anything!"

"You just cut that wire!"

"Humans aren't supposed to know anything about our fieldwork. You're already in a lot of trouble. You think I'm gonna let you know about our ways?"

"Your ways? Look, I know you probably don't trust me but, I'm all alone here. I don't understand anything anymore, why I'm here, how all of you live, and now this. Is this what all of you do?"

"Why should I say anything to you. You killed Voltaire. You escaped prison. You followed me here. I'm kinda surprised you haven't run far from here.

"I know. I'm just so amazed that everything is so different than I thought it would be in your world. It's like being an explorer though I haven't even left Moreco!" The expression on the young vole's face softened as his fascination with this micro-human began to stir.

"Okay, I get it. I dunno how I'd feel in your shoes. So, we were given 'The Field' long ago. All of us do it. We're drawn to it. I really haven't stopped to think why before, now that I think about it."

"You mean this is something all of you do? You damage machines?"

"Yep!", The young vole puffed himself up with a prideful smile, "Always have, always will, it's our job!"

"We've had a running joke about your 'field' work. Humans think there are mythical gremlins that do it. It's mainly a joke. Nobody would ever believe me if I told them it was the voles all along! Why do you do it?"

"Not really sure, to be honest. I don't really care either. It's fascinating work. You should try it sometime! You get a feel for it after a while. My dad taught me everything. This is my first day solo! The science behind sabotage is in play with *the field*. Not just any wire cut will cause problems. If you're an artist, you need to make your work cause intermittent problems, like this wire. If I left it cut and pulled apart, you would only have a dead machine. I have it arranged this way, so the break in the wire will allow electricity to flow and then stop when the wire moves slightly. It really is a lot of fun! Sometimes we sit and watch you people and your frustration with our work. It's even better if we can confuse a serviceman. Once, my Uncle Fred stayed inside a pop machine and kept up his work while the tech tried to figure out the problems. Each time he did, my Uncle would cause another problem just after the tech closed the panels. He would test his work and have to open it up again. Uncle Fred has the record for the most continuous field job at nine hours! He said it was the best day of his life!"

"Well, I don't understand it but, I guess without you and your kind, there would be a lot of hungry servicemen out there."

"Yeah! That's noble right!"

Hello, it's me, the narrator again. I thought I'd mention that these were nice comments by these two. Servicemen like myself don't need a pat on the back every day but, it's nice to be appreciated once in a while. Oh, um, back to the story. Well, I guess I didn't really need to say that but, I gotta finish this thing up so I can get back to work.

The two of them climbed back out of the machine as thirty blinding white flashes occurred. Doug was once again full size, standing next to the jack as he looked down to see a small black shape flash beneath the jack then, out toward the rollup door and beyond. Doug walked back outside and lit up a cigarette, waving just as I pulled away. The narrator me knew what just happened while the real world me drove away with a confused wave and a smile. Neither one of us ever spoke of what we had witnessed. We weren't quite sure if we had a lapse of sanity that day. It was best to keep those thoughts to ourselves. Well, I guess I did let you know about it but, I sure as hell wouldn't let anyone in the real world know!

Perspectives

"How would you describe it then?" she said, becoming more agitated as the conversation lingered, "You really have no idea what you're talking about! I wish you could take my place. One day would be all you would need!" Her tone became increasingly frustrated, faltering between the tears she was attempting to hold back. I was having a hard enough time with this. It was bad enough to have to drag your niece into the office to threaten her with a pink slip. The added emotions were killing me. Candice had been an hour late four times in the last month. Her assemblies were constantly being rejected by Q.C. This was her final warning. I've always demanded compliance to our working hours and the quality of our product. After all, she wasn't carrying her weight, and it made life rough on everyone else.

My familial dilemma established itself six months ago after giving my niece a break with a job. She was in her mid-twenties and recovering from a ravenous heroin addiction at the time. The halfway house she lived in required their residents to be employed or seek a job. It took me less than a second to give her a shot on the line of my small aerospace manufacturing company. Candice had always had a special place in my heart, and it was torture to watch her spiral into addiction. The chance to help her toward a real life was indeed a gift. The work behind the gift was beginning to develop.

"Candice, you're right. I can't understand you. To be honest, I probably wouldn't without being in your shoes! But I have to run this business, and as much as I love you, I can't keep covering for you. This is it, be here on time every day and improve the focus on your work, or I will have to let you go. Believe me, I don't want to have to do that!"

Candice looked away and broke down just as thirty blinding white flashes strobed all around us. Disoriented, I looked up at myself standing next to the table I was once seated at and said with Candice's voice, "What is going on..", hearing her voice verbalizing my thoughts stopped me as my heart began to race. Still staring at myself standing outside of my own body, I noticed that my mouth remained shut while I had been speaking until I heard the words, "I don't know.." from my mouth without my direction of thought. The form before me turned around, looking into the mirror on the wall, and with terror in his voice, announced, "Uncle Dan, This can't be happening! I'm not high. I know I said it but, I don't want you to take my place!" I could hear a genuine concern for me in her/his voice as I sat in disbelief, feeling as though I was within a dream. My body/ Candice walked back to the table and sat down opposite of her body/me. The two of us were unmoored in a state of shock for a full ten minutes. Neither of us spoke. We could do nothing else but look at each other stupidly. I was the first to talk while continuing to be amazed by my new voice, "Well, if this is a dream, I'll wake up soon. Until then, we're going to have to deal with this. Until it wears off, we need to make a plan but, not here. This will get weird quick to everyone else if we stay. I'll follow you to my car."

"Okay, but what do I say if Brad or Charleen stops us on the way out?"

"Just say we'll be back, hell, I don't know.. say your mom, I mean, your sister is sick or something, I don't care. We just have to get outta here." Candice led the way as I noticed she was having difficulty walking like a man when I realized I wasn't doing much better in her body. I hadn't felt this awkward since puberty. We made it out of the building quickly before anyone could stop us, but I noticed a few employees look over at us with puzzled expressions at the sight of our uncoordinated strides. The walk through the plant was terrifying.

Ahead of us was my 1975 Mercedes 450SL convertible. The same car I had bought in high school from a farmer in Texas. It had been sitting in his barn collecting dust for twenty years, and he let me have it for $1500. Over the past twenty years, I have slowly restored her to showroom majesty. I watched as Candice pulled my keys out, ready to hand them over as I cringed while sayin, "No, you better drive. It won't look right otherwise." My face produced a sideways smile as Candice opened the driver's side door and slid into the seat without needing to adjust it or the mirrors. I grabbed the passenger door, once again feeling very strange, never being a passenger in my own car. Candice fired off the engine and backed out of the parking space while I closed my eyes. I had no idea what kind of driver she was, and this was a terrible way of finding out. We turned south down Hardeson, making a right turn on 75th St. She downshifted perfectly to take the steep hill away from the cluster of restaurants at the intersection below. After the plateau, we wound around back downhill as the main Everett Boeing plant came into view. Once again, I felt queasy seeing my primary customer ahead of us. Its size equalling the pit in my stomach. With a left turn south on Seaway Blvd and a merge onto The Boeing Freeway, we made our way toward my house. Another glance northward from The Freeway to The Boeing plant, I saw its gargantuan hangar doors wide open, swallowing a 787, which only furthered my frustration with our dilemma.

Candice made a right onto 84th S.T. S.W. and another to Mukilteo Speedway toward the ferry terminal. We decided to skip my house and go to The Ivars next to the dock. The sky was clear on this autumn early afternoon. A ferry was just pulling from its moorings while a short line of cars, trucks, and semis waited for the next sailing. Candice parked on the street across from Ivars, and both of us exited the car. Once again, my stride, the epitome of weird, at least in my mind. Watching

Candice, I reassured myself, my stride probably looked just as strange to others as it felt to me. We ordered our food and had a seat around the corner allowing for a good view of the waterfront. There were small children running ankle-deep in the water within sprint range of two mothers in a deep conversation while their eyes were glued on their offspring. Both of us sat down at the park bench out of earshot from them.

For some reason, the smell of my fish and chips was much more pronounced. It was varied with many more layers. This was, after all, Candice's sense of smell. She had no idea what a gift it was. I couldn't help but sit there with my paper boat of fish and chips to my nose, drawing in the complexities of aroma. Candice sat staring at me with a blank look in well, my eyes and said once again with my voice,

"What are you doing?"

"I can't believe how much you can smell with this nose! It's like nothing I could ever imagine!"

"Well, don't get too excited Unc, it goes both ways." We tore into our lunch, or I should say I did. Candice did have my sense of taste and smell, and to be honest, I've never been much of a foodie. Now I knew why. I had no ability to take in the joy of taste and smell like I did at this moment. How was it Candice had managed to keep such a nice figure with this kind of ability? Each fry was an event, with its subtle variation of a caramelized outer surface, lightly sprinkled with salt, hypnotic. The fish became a symphony in my, well, Candice's mouth. Conducted expertly between the perfectly fried crust and the delicious fresh cod within. Each bite, an encore of flavor and smell. Candice finished off her small cup of clam chowder, noticing it wasn't anywhere near enough for her man body appetite. I ate half of my meal before realizing I needed to stop as my capacity was at its end. I handed the rest to her, knowing by her/my eyes she was still hungry.

"How are we going to do this, Uncle Dan?" Candice asked with fear showing through my ordinarily stoic face, "I have no idea how to act like a man. Think like a man. Look at me. I can't even eat like a man!" I stopped and looked as she daintily picked up a fry while seated, one leg crossed awkwardly like a woman, back slightly arched forward over her food, while she placed the fry into her mouth and lightly bit off the end.

On the other hand, I noticed that I was sprawled out on the bench, an elbow on either side resting on its back. We were doomed. I quickly changed my position, trying to copy her mannerisms, crossed my leg over the other, and bent slightly toward her as though looking at a freakish mirror. On queue, Candice caught on and tried to take my previous position. Neither of us looked comfortable but, at least we appeared normal.

"Look, we're at the waterfront. There're always people acting weird down here. Nobody cares. You're supposed to have fun in a place like this. We can teach each other here!" she said as though all her answers were given. I couldn't disagree with her as it made the most sense out of any alternative I had been trying to formulate in my head. She finished eating and walked her best man walk to the trash can nearby. I was glad to see she was lightening up a bit now. Both of us walked up and down the sidewalk in front of the benches. First, I coached Candice. I tried to get her to relax and tone down the blatantly, almost cartoon-like masculine strides. After about fifteen minutes, she had a typical gate. Next sitting, which she was able to master quickly. Then, I shook her hand. As I expected, she grasped my hand halfway in just past my fingers and lightly shook. I stopped her, explaining technique, the base of the thumb locked with the base of her/my thumb. A firm, not crushing grip with a light shake. I explained to her not to worry as many men I've encountered don't have this down either.

Next, it was my turn. Candice showed me her walk, reminding me not to work it too much as I wasn't trying to draw eyes. I had no problem agreeing on that point. Sitting, with its many variations, was next in which I was having a difficult time mastering. There was a position where I needed to put one foot under my other leg, and this was somehow comfortable? Over the next few hours, we laughed and practiced our acts. Neither of us felt secure in them but, we were able to appear normal.

We agreed to our work scenarios, I would work on the line building cockpit instrument panels. I had developed the process so, I wasn't concerned about performing the job. To avoid too much conversation with co-workers, I would just say I couldn't talk and point out a future pink slip if I screw up. Candice was relieved to hear she could lock herself in my office and just look at papers if anyone came in. We would go over anything important after work at my house, and she would make those decisions the next day. Candice took me back to her car after everyone else had gone home.

"Uncle Dan, the keys are in my purse!"

"Okay, we'll have to go in and get'm." The production floor was dark and quiet as she walked to her seat on the line and grabbed her purse off the table. She handed it to me, realizing she had forgotten something.

"Make-up, we forgot make-up!"

"Oh crap! I might as well shoot myself!"

"Knock it off; it's gonna be my face, you dweeb!"

"Yeah, I guess you're right."

We followed each other back to my house at about six PM.

"Curfew at the house is at nine Unc so, we've got time. I'm not going to give you much, just mascara and lipstick."

"Okay, let's get this over with." It may have been Candice's body's muscle memory as though on autopilot, her hands completed the task without direction.

"Wow, Unc! It's almost as though you've done this before! Are you leading a double life or something? Should I be looking for feathered boas in your closet?" she said through her/my laughter.

"Nice. Could you imagine that body as a drag queen?" I said while pointing at my six-foot-six frame with its fifty-two-inch

28

jacket size, "I hope never to see anything like that!" We both laughed hysterically, more than likely, half from the thought of my body in drag, the other out of release from the trauma of the day.

I made my way back to her light green 1995 Ford Escort and waved goodbye to my precious niece, who was now waving at me with my hand from the front porch. I got into the old junker, fired up the hesitant engine while being reminded of my youth. My first two or three cars were just like this, and memory came flooding back, both good and bad. I pulled out of the driveway and headed back to Everett to the familiar halfway house I had taken Candice to six months ago. I walked through the door and signed into the logbook beside the door at 8:39. The housemother Jean said hello as she scanned me up and down, making sure I was sober.

"Good to see you home, Candice. Hope you had a good evening; I'm exhausted, long day. Sorry to let you know, Janice came home around 6:00. I found her in her room just after I heard her collapse in her room. She O.D.'d. She's in the hospital now. I'm sorry hun, I know you two were close. I know about all those nights you were up late with her talking. You tried, but, Honey, people choose their own steps." I tried to look stunned about the news of this person I had never met. I had to sell the idea that I cared. I never was able to fake my emotions very well, so I just tried to look shocked. It must have worked as Jean came over and gave me a long hug while stroking my/Candice's hair in comfort.

"I'm so sorry, Jean. I don't know what to say." I really didn't.

"That's okay, Sweetie, we can talk in the morning. I need sleep."

"Okay, sleep good.", I said with Candice's voice. I then realized I had no idea which room was mine. I walked to the first door and looked in to see the room filled with a style of decor nowhere near my niece's tastes, Goth. I moved on to the next room, its door open; a late teens girl in pajamas on her bed looked up saying,

"The hell you looking at?" I was amazed at the inmate attitude, and while stunned, I walked to the last room at the end of the hall. Opening the door, I was relieved to see the familiar sights of all things Candice. I set the alarm for 5:30 AM and got into some pajamas I found on the bed.

Morning came quick as the alarm blared. The girl with the attitude in the next room was pounding on the wall. I shut off the alarm and got dressed. A pair of jeans and a t-shirt. I wasn't willing to wear a dress, even though I/she would look perfectly normal doing so. I managed to get out the door with some toast before the talk Jean had promised. Traffic was light as I pulled into the parking lot at 6:45. I clocked in early and walked to Candice's seat on the production floor. 7:00 AM came as Candice/my body walked up and said,

"Well, how'd it go?"

"No problems. Man, that teenager in the room next to you is hardcore! Oh, I almost forgot, you better sit down."

"What is it?"

"Your friend Janice is in the hospital. She overdosed yesterday in her room." Candice's/my eyes filled with tears as she begged,

"Please let me go to see her. I've been trying to help her for months now. She needs me, Uncle Dan!"

"You're the boss Candice! Go!" I said with a smile watching as my huge body scamper out the door. She had obviously forgotten about everything else but her friend. After she left, I realized she was wearing my skin. Hopefully, she would remember before trying to go into her friend's room. I worked through the morning and took lunch in the break-room finding enough money in Candice's purse for a sandwich, Coke, and a bag of cool ranch-flavored Doritos. Once again, my newfound sense of smell and taste began to amaze while enjoying my meal to the last bite. I was astonished a meal this good could've come from a vending machine. I made my way back to my seat on the floor and finished the panel in front of me, beating my best record.

30

"That was amazing! I've been watching you all day Candice. You've never been this fast!" said Bradley, Candice's co-worker, "I don't think I've seen anyone that fast!"

"I can't lose this job Brad, my uncle came down pretty hard on me yesterday."

"I guess he got through! I was wondering how long you would last around here. Looks like you'll be around for a while!", he shot a weird smile and a wink. I had no response while picking up the completed panel. The last thing in the world I wanted was to respond to his advances. I brought the board to the Q.C. inspection desk and went back to pick up materials to begin a new panel. This time I would try not to stand out. I'd pace myself much slower. While walking back to my seat, I watched Candice/myself walk back to my office. The end of the night came quickly as I continued the work on the third panel of the day. I came to realize the reason I had started this business was coupled with my love for this kind of work. It was like building a puzzle. There was logic behind every connection. The wire and cable routing had to be done with precision, not only for a professional look but for ease of service if a technician ever needed to work on the panel. I was halfway through the third panel when I realized the shift was over.

Candice/my body came to the door of my office and called out, "Candice, I'd like to see you in my office, please." More looks from my co-workers as I gathered Candice's belongings and walked back to my office. It was a surreal moment halfway across the production floor as a thought hit me while I was still trying to grasp how to operate this contraption I was trapped in. It was a thought I had before in theory yet, now I was keenly aware of its airtight, concrete reality.

We are spirit and soul within a machine made of flesh. It is a beautifully complex instrument designed to experience life and observe creation.

While struggling with the controls of another's vehicle, I was also aware of how each vehicle can discern the complexities of those experiences in varied ways. A person born blind wouldn't have the reference we do of the variations of the color red. The definition of color is another issue none of us can really know to be the same as the person next to us. If I was looking at a bluebird learning its hue to be blue, you could call what you see red the color blue. If there is consensus upon a hue's name when it is presented, this by no means can equate with what our eyes see. It merely names that experience. I was able to see a massive difference in my sense of smell and taste while in Candice's body. The theory of varied experience in color's definitions didn't show up but, I still wouldn't be surprised if it could be active in other people.

I walked into my office, shut the door, and sat down in front of my desk. Candice smiled and asked, "Well, how'd it go?"

"It actually went well. It's been a while since I've built a panel. It was kinda fun! How bout you?

"Well, after I got to the hospital and gave my name at the front desk, I realized by the look the nurse gave me I wasn't going to see Janice. The nurse must have thought Candice was a unisex name like Leslie or Carrol cause she let me know Janice was recovering and would be released tomorrow morning."

"That's great! What about the rules at your house?"

"I'm not sure. I know if we're found using, we can get kicked out. I have no idea if they give warnings or if you just get kicked out. I guess we'll see. If she does come back to the house, you're going to have to try to keep coaching her. She needs the support, especially after this." Candice spent the next half hour coaching me on the ins and outs of addiction and how to support Janice.

As she spoke about the drug's pull upon an addict, I began to feel Candice's body yearn for what I had no reference of. It was the strangest feeling knowing this device I was occupying almost had a mind of its own. I was glad that I was unable to fulfill its desires. I had no knowledge of where to begin to find what it wanted, and knowing firsthand this body wasn't mine made it much easier to disengage from its longings. This experience helped me to become much more empathetic toward those caught in addiction. I was overwhelmed with thankfulness to know the division between its desires and the will of my own spirit. A sea-change had occurred in my perception of the struggles of addiction but, more importantly, the victories my niece had achieved. She was fighting a powerful adversary and succeeding. What I had thought was laziness regarding her tardiness was actually admirable behavior mixed with exhaustion. She was too honorable to admit her late-night counseling of her friend as an excuse. This gave me a reason to respect her all the more.

Over the next two weeks, Candice continued to coach me on how to encourage her friend. Janice was given a severe warning when she returned to gather her belongings and allowed to continue her residence. I tried my best to help Janice, but, to be honest, I felt as though I was an imposter. I did my best, and I think I pulled it off for the most part. I tried to get home at curfew and spent as much time in Candice's room as possible. I would make excuses like being tired or feeling sick. That said, I did attempt to help Janice. There were at least two occasions when I tried to repeat Candice's words. The small understanding of the body's longing for the drug did help me to relate to Janice so, I guess it wasn't a complete sham.

During the same timeframe, it came to my attention that Candice had a leadership aptitude and business sense. I began to explain the administration side of the company to her. She astonished me as she caught on quickly to many aspects of the trade. Everything from client interaction, projected trends, employee management to the natural gift of an entrepreneurial mind. As the weeks passed, I actually loosened the reigns a bit to see what would happen. I was pleasantly surprised as she had chosen to change suppliers for some of the semiconductors, paint, and raw materials. The changes she made will produce substantial gains for the company.

I decided to take my body to lunch to celebrate her accomplishments. We arrived at the Mukilteo Ivar's once again, this time on an overcast day. Candice parallel parked my car near the restaurant just as there were thirty blinding white flashes all around us. My hands gripped the wheel in front of me as both of us yelled at the top of our lungs with relief. We then sat there once again, looking at each other stupidly for a few minutes. The surreal once again took hold as both of us regained our original forms. Familiar yet, with a slight awkwardness that lasted the rest of the day. Once again, my sense of smell and taste had returned to normal, yet, like a phantom limb, I was still able to piece together what I was missing.

We discussed many things that day that produced dramatic change for both of us. Candice went on to return to school. She got her MBA from the University of Washington and began to make her presence known naturally in our company. I, being the president and founder, was able to do what I had enjoyed the most. I reasserted myself as chief of R&D while continuing as CEO. My confidence in Candice allowed me to focus on the joys of my job again. My stress levels decreased after integrating into the best fit for my work life. Candice continued to succeed, helping to lead our company toward higher profits and increasing job opportunities for many fortunate people.

I am now retired, a late bloomer to the married life. My wife Margret and I have been together for fifteen years, two years after my strange experience walking in someone else's shoes. I like to think those three weeks have made me a better husband but, the truth is, while I try my best, men and women are vastly different in the best ways possible. The mystery of these differences and how they materialize is one of the most fascinating things in life's journey I've experienced while in my own   *contraption.*

Lyrics

There was a time a few years back when I decided to stop listening to music. I had been a fanatical listener for most of my life, from my childhood years onward. I honed my tastes in music, enjoying everything from Mozart to The Clash depending upon my mood. I found digging for the unknown to be an enjoyable pass time. Underground bands had become amongst my favorites. I had a feeling like a gold miner would after finding a nugget in a riverbed. The joy of that find lasting a season or more was amplified for some reason, knowing I was enjoying something away from the masses. My taste in a sound was a complex mix of beat, style, and lyrics. The cleverer the lines, the better, or the mood exuded verbally. The genre had little draw if the right combinations were lacking.

While working on some architectural drawings for a client, I listened to the song "The Field" by a band called "The Voles." I became lost in thought over the frightening storyline being told.

These are the lyrics:

It's not what you think, don't go like that
I'm afraid you're mistaken bout the life we got
Never should've found out now
Shouldn't know the truth
Can't help the fact
But you've lost your youth

Tell me the lie one more time
Give into the false

35

Speak illusions once more
Or prepare for loss

Shine the light here, and you'll regret
Open the floodgates to know the threat
Uncover the hidden, oh shame on you
Disclose mystery. We'll come for you

Just then, thirty blinding white flashes occurred within my office as I was putting the finishing touches on the blueprints for a new Moreco planned on the other side of town. I had no idea why but, I was now within the storyline of the song's lyrics. I don't know how but, I knew I had uncovered a conspiracy within the mainstream music business' corporate structure. This was similar to how tobacco corporations had been disrobed in the late nineties for using non-tobacco additives designed to cause addiction in consumers. The music industry was found to perpetuate political and social directives designed to corrupt society. There was no need for the subliminal messages experimented within the seventies. A continual message mixed with lies was all that was needed. The funny thing was that Adolph Hitler was the one who originally made mention of this kind of conditioning. The masses, addicted to their favorite songs, had no idea of the way they were being manipulated.

I had in my possession a flash drive with corporate directives and agreements between major labels to dispense them. It wasn't long before government agents associated with the conspiracy were on to me. The Voles song "The Field" rang in my head as I escaped the first of many assassination attempts. I was in my apartment contemplating my findings when the first of five blasts through my fifteenth story window changed my life forever. They were different from the movies. There was no gunshot sound, merely faint glass breaks and thuds into the wall behind me. I hit the ground after the third impact, realizing what was happening.

The days turned into months, then years, as my savings dwindled while on the run from my pursuers. I had no way of continuing the run. The reporters I attempted to meet with wouldn't touch my story or its evidence. After every contact with the media, the attempts on my life increased. The money was running out. My zigzag across the country landed odd jobs, dishwashing, and fry cook positions, which I was thankful for. In the end, I gave up and destroyed the flash drive just as thirty blinding white flashes occurred. I squinted and opened my eyes to see myself in my office. The new Moreco plans were in front of me on my desk. This parallel version of myself was oblivious to my observation and his own predicament. Though the situation was confusing to me at the time, I was unable to intervene with him in any way. I stared helpless at myself while in an almost psychedelic state of wonder. Behind him upon the shelf sat a set of speakers belching out "The Field" by the Voles.

An Exchange

He was a disappointed, bitter man who spent his days focused on his failure. The only thing that gave him solace was turning his attention toward his hatred of the humanity around him. The details of their shortcomings amplified in his mind seemed to overshadow any empathy he may have been wise to give. Over time his obsession with these thoughts overtook his life. It was unclear why; it may have been a shield, a way to avoid his own issues.

Hugo fumed as his coworker Jared again upstaged his best efforts to advance within the small software firm. Jared, a naturally gifted coder, made it a point to call attention to any and all flaws within the code. It wasn't merely a concern for the product. He specifically brought issues to management, not taking the high ground and discussing them with coworkers first.

The project had been inspired by Hugo's idea of a mapping algorithm for the suppliers and consumers of the food industry in China. His blueprint had been adopted by the firm and was a few months away from its reveal date. Hugo had signed overall intellectual property to the firm. To begin with, he had been excited. The limelight was good and raises sufficient. As things progressed, the company hired superstars with egos to match. Jared was the worst example of the attitude he loathed about these new hires. They usually had no respect for anyone but themselves. This was just another day of humiliation generated by Jared's big mouth and persuasive charisma.

That night, Hugo began his plans. After eight years coding for Imagine Corp., the last two under self-made oppression, he decided he wanted revenge. Dialing the ticket outlet for the nearby Charles Theater, he calmly placed the receiver to his ear.

"Yes, I would like three tickets to the show this Friday."

The response, on the other end,

"Okay, do you have a seating preference, Sir?"

"I would like two seats together and another anywhere you have a single open seat, please."

"I have two seats in the center section, row fifteen, seats eight and nine for $55.00 each, and the single-seat at in the same section in the last row for $55.00. Will that work for you, Sir?"

"That will be fine. I would like to pick them up at will call."

Hugo left his apartment and picked up the tickets down the street before returning home to begin a list of supplies. Everything would need to be ready in two days. He grabbed his list and made his way out the door to do some shopping. First, a stop at the army surplus on Wexler Ave. He walked to the glass case near the back of the store. The man behind the counter seemed to be an early sixties veteran with a battle-worn face holding many difficult memories.

"I'd like to see that one." Hugo pointed at the long blade near the end of the case.

"This one's a World War One Belgium army bayonet. Pretty rare. I've only seen two others like it. Are you a collector?"

"I think I will become one today," he said as the salesman handed him the weapon. The sixteen-inch blade, an awkward weapon without being attached to a rifle, felt strange in Hugo's hands. "I'll take it."

"Cash or credit?"

Walking out of the shop, he deposited the blade in his trunk and then made his way to the hardware store. The evening progressed without event as the passions within his mind began to become unmanageable. That night he needed a second sleeping pill to push away his thoughts.

The following day Hugo made his way to work as a feeling of glee overtook him. He actually took the time to look his best before leaving home for the office.

"Hi, Jared! I wanted to thank you for all of your input on the code. I bought you two tickets to The Voles this Friday night."

"How did you know they were my favorite band? That's awesome, thanks, Hugo!" Hugo had spent weeks researching social media and was pleased that Jared was too stupid to figure it out. It was only a matter of time now. He watched as Jared walked to the coffee kiosk and stopped himself from staring at his victim while trying to change the demented expression on his face.

Friday arrived, the workday rocketed by as Jared walked out the door, flashing the tickets in the air with thanks to Hugo on his way out. The thrill Hugo's mind conceived was hypnotic. It was as though he was no longer within his own body. He would need to work fast now. An inaudible twisted giggle within himself moved him out the door toward his goal.

He checked into a cheap hotel across the street from the theater. Leaving the lights off, he peered out the window at the crowd forming on the road below. Ten minutes elapsed as he spied Jared and a friend arrive in the line just as the doors opened. Hugo put on his coat and grabbed his own ticket and walked out the door.

Arriving at the end of the line, he joined the last five people entering the building. He walked through the length of the lobby and entering the theater, a run-down excuse for a showhouse, a ruin of its previous splendor. Taking his seat at the back, he kept his eye on Jared three rows up, seated next to his date. She, too, had been a fool. Posting her cell number in her profile online, the plan was too easy.

Before the band took the stage, Hugo walked back outside and dialed Amanda, Jared's date. He explained to her that it would be fun to surprise Jared with a party celebrating his accomplishments. He asked her to keep it a secret and asked her to come outside for a second so he could give details and point out the location across the street. There would be many coworkers waiting as well.

Amanda walked to the lobby as Hugo pulled her into a janitor's closet while holding an ether-soaked rag to her face. He then gagged and tied her up comfortably within the closet. He actually felt bad, not wanting to harm her in the least. She was merely a means to an end. He then returned to the concert as the band was greeting the crowd.

"Hi Jared, I didn't want you to be bothered by knowing I was here too but, I just saw your girlfriend leave with another guy!"

"What! What the hell! What'd he look like?"

"Tall, mid-twenties, dark hair, loaded. They went across the street. I actually saw the room from the sidewalk. I can show you."

"Bastard! Let's go. Of all the times to go! She knows this is my favorite band!" The group began their first song. It started slowly and began to build to a frenzy as Hugo and Jared walked out the door. The sound matching Hugo's nervously excited heartbeat. They crossed the street in the light rain, making their way to the entrance.

"Follow me. They're on the third floor." Hugo took the stairs as Jared kept up. Just before opening the third-story stairwell exit, Hugo, a much more powerful man than Jared's willowy frame, turned and took a full-force swing at his unsuspecting victim. The punch connected at Jared's temple, knocking him unconscious as he slumped into a pile on the landing.

Hugo calmly opened the door of the stairwell, finding no witnessing eyes. He then picked up his younger coworker and walked across the hall to his room. He made sure to gag and bind the focus of his hatred, then sat down in a chair across the room to wait. An hour passed as Hugo could no longer control his own will. All resistance was removed. The only thing within was the perverted desire to kill. All focus rested upon this. It was euphoric and worth the wait.

Hugo opened his bag, retrieving the bayonet, and began to sharpen it with the same whetstone he had used for several days. It was a long razor now, unlike when purchased from the surplus store. The Band-Aids on Hugo's fingers were a testament to the fact that in his insanity-fueled pleasure of honing the blade, he had inadvertently cut himself several times. Strangely this only fueled the joy of his sickness.

Jared awoke slowly with confusion. His eyes eventually analyzing his surroundings with an understanding of his plight as his gagged nonverbal pleadings began to fill the room. Hugo opened the window enough to let in the sound of Jared's favorite band's closing song mute his victim's unintelligible beg for mercy. Hugo walked over to him, threw him off of the chair onto the floor. He loomed over Jared with crazy eyes and the longest knife Jared had ever seen.

Hugo sat atop him with dominance as he slowly inserted the blade beneath Jared's ribcage into his chest cavity. The bayonet punctured a lung before entering the left ventricle of his heart while Jared writhed in pain. There was a twist of the blade just as thirty blinding white flashes filled the room.

Hugo was shocked, now tied, gagged and a bayonet intruding his chest. Above him, Jared pulled the blade out. He reinserted the tool on the opposite side under Hugo's ribs toward his heart with wild eyes. The pain seared through him from head to toe, originating from the entry wounds. He lay there listening to the sound of his murderer's favorite band come from the open window. Shock began to settle in from the pain as the life seeped out of him onto the floor.

Thirty blinding white flashes occurred once again as Hugo found himself at the surplus store. He pulled the blunt, rusty weapon out of his bag, setting it on the counter to the storekeeper's surprise.

"You want to return it so soon? It's only been a half-hour?"

"Yeah, I've had a change of mind. I don't think it's me anymore."

"Well, I can't give you the full price back. How's $150?"

"That's fine, thanks."

Hugo walked back to the office just before the end of his lunch break. Coincidentally, Jared passed him in the stairwell.

"Hey, Hugo! Up for a game of poker tonight, I've got some buddies from college in town, and it would be great to introduce you to them."

"Sure, Jared, that would be great."

"Cool, be at my place at 7:30!"

"Okay, I'll see ya there!"

Hugo walked back to his desk and began rechecking the code for inaccuracies while listening to his favorite band, "The Voles," through his headphones.

Ghost

I have to get this out for my own sanity's sake. The confidentiality agreements I've signed with DARPA and my Top-Secret security clearance with the US government be dammed! My conscience is all I care about now at my age! I've kept this to myself for twenty years now. Even my wife and kids had no idea what I did at work. They understood my situation and never pressed me on the subject. When asked, they told others about my profession- *Dad goes to work, makes copies all day, and comes home.* Little did they know the truth associated with their flippantly sarcastic description of the life I was immersed in.

My research began with a hypothesis I had postulated for my doctorate thesis in nuclear science and engineering while at M.I.T. In layman's terms: Matter is composed of an arrangement of atoms with spaces in between those atoms. If there was a way to calibrate two different bodies of matter perfectly, in theory, the calibrated bodies could physically pass through each other without disruption to either subject.

The government snatched me up as soon as my tassel was turned. Still a young man of thirty years, I embarked on a journey bloated with self-confidence, flattered by the interest given me by the defense department. My days and nights were self-motivated isolation to the research wing I was assigned to in Arlington. I cannot disclose the true identities of those associated with my work so, I will use pseudonyms. It took me a year to prove myself and my theories as a viable candidate for funding before I was given my own department and research assistants.

The project was given the code name 'Ghost,' and we were allowed a substantial budget. Our wing was fitted with a small particle accelerator roughly the size of a gymnasium. My assistants ranged in function: nuclear physicists, mechanical engineers, biologists, geneticists, to name a few. The project began after three years of research. Plans were laid for the 'calibrators,' as we called them, and construction began. Another three years passed as the 'calibrators' were completed and placed in series with the particle accelerator. We were ready to start.

The first subjects for calibration were rats *thousands of rats*. My heart toward the white rodents eventually hardened after the first two hundred subjects were eviscerated instantly as the calibrators were adjusted. I've never been partial to rats but, the sight of them imploding before my eyes for the first few weeks of tests was disturbing. I was amazed at how the poor things tugged at my heart. We probably would have stopped sooner if not for each subject's apparent partial success in alignment. The first three had untouched regions of their bodies postulated to be the result we were looking for. A foot here, a snout there, in retrospect, it didn't seem like enough evidence to press on but, our motivations were set.

Late in 2056, two years after we had begun testing on live subjects, we reached a breakthrough. After the precise calibration of two test subjects with one another, my theory was justified. Two very expensive rats frolicked together within a clear polymer box amongst the Timothy hay, unaware of their significance. The two rats, when touching, passed through each other without incidence or notice. One would overshadow and seem to disappear into the other from time to time. This was the first time I saw my theory become a reality, and though it all made sense to me mathematically, to see it before my eyes was, well, disturbing. I sat and observed those two rats for hours as they ran around their box, commingling at random intervals. It was surreal, almost frighteningly so, knowing each one of their atoms was perfectly spaced to be able to pass through the others.

Eventually, the directives were passed down from the powers leading the project. We were instructed to begin the necessary preliminary steps toward using this technology for human soldiers. I was a fool not to have expected this to become a required command from The Defense Department. I guess my mind was so focused on my goals, I never really thought about the moral and ethical issues. To combat my fears, I decided to take the point position in the next step of our research, even to the extent of demanding that I would be the first to be exposed to calibration.

"You ready, professor? The lab technician Judy Peace called out nervously. It had only been six months from the first rat success. During this period, the laboratory had successfully calibrated hundreds of dogs and monkeys in addition to the pioneering rodents. These subjects were paired not only with animals but also with random animate and inanimate objects. They had decided to tune all lifeforms to the same frequencies once adjusted to their own baselines. Eventually, it became clear there was no need to use pairs of subjects. The calibrations could be tuned to anything within the environment targeted. Judy ground her teeth subconsciously while waiting for my reply.

"I'm ready, Judy. Hit me!" The accelerator came online after Judy's keyboard initiations, the howling low hum filling the building.

As an observer of the effects of our work, I previously noticed very minor physical issues during the calibration process. Being the subject was an entirely different matter. As the calibrator's cathodes began to receive their supply charges from the accelerator, every hair on my body stood on end just before I was changed. Without understanding, I witnessed the calibrator's exposure aperture open in slow motion. It was curious as I saw what should have been two-thousandths of a second opening to be what seemed to be taking thirty seconds.

I decided to yell out to Judy to abort the experiment, but my own voice was leaving my mouth in a wave pattern so slow I could feel its fluctuations as lethargic morse code like thuds. While I was distracted by this experience, I was shocked by an equally opposite phenomenon. Thirty blinding white flashes strobed all around before the calibrator's beam even left the exposure aperture. This was another detail I missed earlier; the calibrator's beam had a vibrant pink tone. It was almost a slap in the face as though a reminder of the dead rats. Curiously, these events dragged on for what seemed like an eternity to me. A nano-second elapsed after the white flashes had completed before I was hit with the pink beam of energy.

I actually felt the separation/calibration of atoms within my body. Knowing by first-hand knowledge what was happening on a sub-atomic scale did nothing to calm my fears. Then, it was over. I felt normal again, just like I would imagine my rats would have.

"You okay!" Judy yelled out, unable to contain her fear.

"Yes, I think I am. I guess we'll see what happens next." I replied as I walked toward the nearest wall.

"Here it goes," I said while bracing myself for the collision with the cinderblock boundary before me. Then, I felt nothing more than a subtle, rough, concrete brushed feeling within myself as I passed through it. It was akin to swimming or feeling a breeze. I stopped and looked at Judy. We were both speechless.

I completed my subsequent tests within the confines of what we had calibrated to my body. It was a city block's worth of space. Walking outside the lab, I passed through trees, buildings, a cat, and quickly through an unsuspecting pedestrian who was preoccupied with thought. Each experience was slightly different, having its own smells and texture if I lingered within the substance. I was fascinated and terrified equally yet, not enough to conclude my tests. I reached the calibration's boundary and was then stopped as any ordinary mortal would be.

As time and our experiments progressed, we were directed to expand the range of the calibrated areas and the calibrated subjects. In a joint directive with HARP, the specifications and effect of calibration could be sent anywhere in the world.

I decided I needed insurance from the government who now owned my research and its active components. I entered the lab one night and keyed in the necessary credentials and coordinates to enable freedom of movement throughout the northern hemisphere. The process took hours as the uplink transferred to and from HARP. Once all the data was logged within the lab's system, I hit the initiate sequence and rushed down to the "change floor," as we began to call it. The same experience occurred without the initial thirty blinding white flashes. From that point on, my life was forever changed.

Just before making this decision, I had decided to leave my research behind. The news had been filled with stories of significant changes within the governments of the world. Numerous leaders of those nations belligerent toward the west quickly began either to comply or were found to be mysteriously missing. I knew what was going on. My work was the source. Though it seemed to be a tremendous advantage on the surface, I began to speculate how this technology could be used for evil. I wasn't convinced it hadn't already, as I was never politically minded.

My disappearance was not unnoticed. After a month, my wife and children were taken from our home. While on the run, I checked in with a colleague who informed me of their abductions. The government made no attempt to hide its actions to encourage me to come out of hiding. I decided to take issues into my own hands.

Over the last twenty years, I have sought to locate my family. I admit there were seasons that I just gave up. Those were the instances when a new clue would push me back into the fight.

The main advantage I had was that our work had one safeguard, myself. I, being absent from the calibration process, halted all continued "changes." Unfortunately, I could not be absolutely certain this was a foolproof assurance.

Last month I found them. My wife was amazed to see me alive, thinking I was killed in an experiment 20 years ago. The authorities had fabricated a story to allow them to believe they were in danger. My children, now adults, had very little memory of me. It wasn't until I demonstrated my abilities to them and explained the ramifications did, they take me seriously. Their lives had moved on. I had been missing or dead to them for two decades. My wife had remarried. The lifelong search for my missing family was bittersweet. I was relieved to know they were alive and thriving. I was heartbroken I was no longer a component of their lives.

After this loss, I was hardened thoroughly. I began to seek the powers within the government that had driven my project. I needed to get answers to why I had been blackballed. The long road of seeking a resolution began.

When my detective work began, I lived in a small studio apartment above a bar in the hill country outside Austin, Texas. This was a completely different kind of study than I was familiar with. Mapping atomic structures and their corresponding voids curiously resembled the type of flowchart-based logical analysis I initiated to locate my targets. Months went by as I homed in, past the conspicuous people I had as contacts when the project was operational. They were nothing more than expendable lackeys. The night of the event seemed to highlight that not only was I close, but this was getting dangerous.

I entered a code name to locate a suspected personal residence G.P.S. coordinate of an undersecretary of the C.I.A. into a dark web search engine. My laptop labored with the query until I started to think I had made a mistake with my choice of sites. An hour went by before the result page appeared with a strange response. The page was bright florescent green with the word "Don't" in the center of the screen. I returned to my desk and stared at the laptop for ten minutes as my imagination of fears played out full-color movies in my mind. I was sweating, and my heart was racing as I began to pound the keyboard to try to get the website to release my computer. It was too late. The laptop caught fire in front of me as my panic level doubled. I ran for a fire extinguisher and put out the small blaze that had started to ignite the furniture. Running to my room, I began to pack my duffel bag, a choice of luggage I had made years prior. As I left my apartment, I saw a familiar black S.U.V.s at the bottom of the hill down the street. I had a slight advantage as my view of their vehicles was from at least five miles away.

I made it to my car- a 2004 Mercury Marauder. I had chosen this vehicle mainly due to its drab exterior. Looking like the most boring car someone could buy was key to its sleeper personality. I had the engine modified from the standard high-performance levels off the showroom floor. A speed shop across town added the twin turbos making it the ugliest land yacht rocket known to man.

My duffel, a sleeping bag, and a few odds and ends made it into the truck before I left the parking lot. I decided to drive casually before turning onto the highway to not attract attention from any possible witness. I hit the Mopac expressway heading north, and gravity overtook my right foot. At first, I was just like any other Austin driver making a beeline to the fast lane. The downward forces pulled the sole of my foot into the floorboard. The other cars around me suddenly appeared to stop as I weaved through them as though making a tapestry. It was becoming real work to keep from hitting these obstacles. I glanced down at my speedometer and found I was passing 160 MPH. All my senses were alive as I was in the latter half of the fight or flight mode.

I turned west on the 45-toll road until I hit 183 North. Luckily my run was before the rush hour but, the slow, law-abiding cars continued to block my path. East of Liberty Hill, 183 ceased being a divided highway and became more of a change for safety at the speed I was traveling. I slowed to the speed limit and found a farm-to-market road heading toward Lake Buchanan.

I neglected to check my fuel gauge until this point and found I was on an eighth of a tank. Fortunately, I found a small gas station just up the road and pulled over to fill up. With the tank full and a bag full of gas station food, I resumed my escape. After about ten miles, I decided to pull over again into what appeared to be a shuttered row of empty warehouses.

Driving to the receiving dock at the back of the second building, I parked and shut off the engine. The radio was useless for an update on if I was a focus in any way. Was I just paranoid? Could my laptop have just burned up coincidently? I was starting to question myself as I tore open a packaged sandwich wrapper. Realizing I was famished, the mustard and mayo packs were neglected as I wolfed down the disgusting meal. While finishing more snacks, it began to get dark. At once, fatigue overtook me so, I grabbed my sleeping bag and got into the backseat. The dry winter air crept into the car as I slept off and on through the night.

It was evident to me in the morning that I had made a mistake by running. Before sunrise, I fired up the engine and let it warm up while eating some stale donuts and a cold bottled coffee, another gourmet gas station delight. I cranked the heat on and pulled back onto the road heading back home.

Five miles into my return trip, I spotted three black S.U.V.s conspicuously one after the other in the oncoming lane. Looking in my rear-view mirror, I witnessed all three pull high-speed U-turns heading my way. My initial thoughts resumed as I buried my foot into the accelerator. They had no chance of catching up to me as long as I could keep all four wheels on the blacktop. My speedometer was reading close to 160 again when I saw the helicopter overhead. I was surprised to notice this wasn't what most would describe as a "black ops" chopper. This was a blacked-out Bell Invictus attack fighter.

I began to slow the car as soon as I saw a batch of office buildings. The chopper followed. I caught sight of a laser beam just before I turned into the parking lot. Immediately, the green aiming beam was replaced by a red beam that cut off the rear half of the car. I went into a harsh spin-stop without rear wheels before I leaped through the driver's door toward the nearest building. I passed into the closest wall and made my way into the basement. I decided to stay within the wall to keep from being found.

I could hear the chopper landing outside and car tires squealing to a stop a few minutes later. My heart was racing as I heard what sounded like a small army of agents and spec ops personnel overtake the building. Those occupying the business I had chosen were audibly in chaos over what was transpiring. The only option I had was to keep quiet within the wall.

An hour elapsed as every joint in my body became cramped as I waited. The chopper started up again just before the three SUVs left the parking lot. I risked leaving my camouflage to the joy of my frozen joints. The building residents were escorted to their vehicles near the beginning of the siege, so I was free to leave.

Suspecting that intelligence personnel had been left behind to run surveillance, I decided to stay within the building for as long as it took to make sure I wasn't being tailed. That decision locked me into that building for a month.

That time was the strangest experience. I lived off rations of breakroom leftovers and vending machine cuisine. Several times over those weeks, I needed to suppress belly laughs over some of the conversations I heard. Accusations of stolen lunches, questions about why and how the vending machines' inventories were out of phase with the charges stored in the logs. The vending machine company was threatening to remove their source of revenue. The manager who was given the unlikely task of dealing with the vendor did his best to be understanding yet, firmly denied responsibility. Many wondered why certain foods were cleaned out of the machines while others were untouched.

The talk continued beyond the subject of breakroom food to a subdued rumor of The Jacobs Company's own "Ghost." The missing food only started these theories. Out of boredom, I began to rearrange a few things within the office here and there. On one of my more motivated projects, I moved the supplies closet to the other side of the building, carefully arranging everything exactly as it was in the original cabinet. The office staff became highly frustrated after the third move. My final supplies transfer was deposited on Alice Janus' desk. I had determined her to be the winner of the most irritating complainer award (This was my own invention). The mound of products four feet high was still perfectly organized yet, teetering.

On my final day, a Friday, I left the building after the staff left for the weekend. I couldn't help but feel paranoid after venturing out of my fortress. I made it two miles down the road toward the next small town on the highway when I saw an unmarked car similar to what an agent would drive pull over just past the driveway from the building I had left. I didn't know what to do so I ran. My fears were confirmed as the car pulled out at high speed toward my location.

This was when an idea came to me, *just go down!* Why hadn't I thought of this before? This brings up the uncanny aspects of being calibrated. The experience comes with resistance to the environment you're in. It takes an act of will to move through something. We decided early on that if we calibrated the environment too freely, like the rats that passed through each other in the lab, things would get too chaotic. The resistance was hard to describe, similar to wet cement, yet you could move through it with the right motivation.

I descended into the earth below me after leaving the road and ducking behind a tree. I felt the soil, rocks, even the roots of the tree as I pulled myself lower. My instincts screamed at me to stop, and I quickly realized why. Being inside the void within a wall may be a claustrophobic experience yet, there's ample oxygen. The ground enveloped my head, and I at once learned my limitation. I quickly ascended back to the surface. I found a length of PVC pipe on the ground about two hundred yards away, to my surprise and relief. I could hear the car pull off the road with gravel under its tires. Using the pipe, I quickly went underground again, using the pipe as a snorkel. After half an hour elapsed, I moved back to the surface.

While I ascended back above ground, thirty blinding white flashes strobed all around me. I found myself staring into a plexiglass box, the two small lab rats that had confirmed my theories long ago. Immediately, I then attempted to pass through the table supporting the container. I was met with a natural resistance that had an overwhelming emotional effect upon me. A joy overtook me that carried me to destroy as much of my research as I could. I had to wait until the entire staff left for the night before destroying documents and sabotaging the machines.

That night, I found my wife and children at home, in peace. I made the decision to take them with me into a life of obscurity from that day on. We crossed the Canadian border on foot later that week. Since that day, we have been living off-grid in small rural towns on both sides of the border. This way of life has been a sacrifice but, knowing the alternative, it's a blessing.

A Choice

"There comes a time in your life when you need to pay attention to what's really going on."

"That sounds profound and all but, whadda ya mean?" he countered with a confused tone in his voice and an expression to match. The last month had been filled with these kinds of ambiguous words. The apprentice had tried hard to be respectful. In truth, he wanted to understand the wisdom the old one had been dispensing.

"It's not about you. It's not about me. We are players, and yet, if we focus on ourselves, we will miss everything."

"I'm sorry, Sir but, you're leaving everything so open-ended, I can't figure out anything you're saying. I mean no disrespect; I just don't get it!"

The old one smiled. It had been decades since anyone from this generation had taken the time to seek wisdom. In fact, visitors to his humble cottage had dwindled down to only a handful over the last twenty years. The value of Truth had diminished in this age. Still, this young man was an encouragement to the old sage. Incredible knowledge was commonplace in this era yet, wisdom was a rare hidden gem most forgot about. It was out of fashion, like a piece of jewelry that had gone out of style. The old one watched as a drone patrol unit passed overhead like a massive dragonfly. It sped away to the southeast on its way back to the city beyond the sea of tree-covered rolling hills. He turned back to the apprentice and calmly replied, knowing the young man's frustration.

"Son, you're coming to the end of your own understanding. This is a good sign. I am limited, and I cannot breach your borders. You have come to seek Truth yet; I am not its fountain. I am merely a fellow traveler at your side drinking from the same well. You thirst for what you're unfamiliar with. The longing of your heart can only be satisfied by the One who bestows the gift.

"So, I can't learn anything more from you, Sir? Are you saying I've wasted my time here? I've put everything on hold, hoping you could give me some answers!" The young man became desperate. "I can't go on without having purpose. The mundane would be bearable if I had a reason to endure it. Please show me a way! Who is The One?"

"Son, purpose is in the hand of The One who created *the purpose* of purpose. I would suggest asking the One who has many names, all of which lead to his character and the fact that He Is. The Eternal is the only one who can give you what you desire." After hearing the ancient prophet speak these words, the young man was struck with their power. He decided to heed the old man and closed his eyes while seated across the table from him. He remembered the old one saying a few weeks back that The Eternal was spirit. He was outside of time. He knew all. The sage had explained this Omnipotent One was a triune deity. The Father, The Son, The Holy Spirit. They were co-equal persons. They were One God, a quality beyond human comprehension. The young man remembered the older's explanation that The Son had left glory to live a human life in order to sacrifice it for those He wished to give eternal life. They would need their iniquities removed. Their best had failed to accomplish this on their own. The Son was their only salvation. The young man realized immediately that he had heard the elder's words on this topic but was unmoved until now.

All at once, the young man was overwhelmed by his own lack. The knowledge of his sins over the span of his life. Sins committed by thought, word, and deed. He realized even what most would consider minor offenses had their root in a heart that had missed the mark. That target was the way, the blueprint that the Creator had drawn. The young man was without excuse. He knew his need. The old one had explained a few weeks ago that The Creator's blueprint was the perfect way to live but, He used that plan to lead man to His salvation. He understood those instructions were unable to save men from eternal death. The blueprint would need to be walked by the Savior, who would also be The Sacrifice for those unable to live it sufficiently to gain eternal life. By faith, the old one explained the forgiveness preceded a life that came to know and follow the blueprint of The Heart of The Creator.

The words of the old one echoed in the mind of the younger- *The Eternal is the only one who can give you what you desire.* He reached out with faith to The Eternal, praying inwardly to Him-

Eternal Father, I need the salvation this old man has spoken of. I need the sinless blood shed by your Son to remove my sin. I need purpose. I need You. As the young man finished his last words, there were thirty blinding white flashes. The young man was unsure if the older had experienced the same event but, he was too distracted to notice. Every word uttered by the sage became crystal clear. He had seen that the prayer he had spoken was fueled by wisdom. It was clear the Third Member of the Trinity- The Holy Spirit had quickened his understanding just before he prayed. Before the knowledge of his own salvation took hold after the thirty blinding white flashes, the young man had been led by The Spirit of Wisdom to pray. He looked up at the old one as tears streamed down his own cheeks while looking at a young man in the elder's place. Gone was the deep topography of wrinkles on his face. He was now a dearly loved brother. The old man smiled once again, sensing the change in the younger.

The two began a new journey together through eternity as members of the same family. The younger began living a life of reliance upon the Savior to finish His work within him. He was moved to live his life as an honor to The Almighty. There were uncounted failures mixed with the mercy needed to walk the road home. The younger learned what the old one had known; life was a succession of surrender. Surrender toward the better choice. The decisions aimed at honor toward The Eternal and the ones created in His image. It was a kind of continuous death. Death to a life of self. In exchange, a life filled with peace, even in trial, and hope for the reward of choices turned away from selfishness.

Ten thousand years had passed since the return of King Jesus. He had defeated the enemy of mankind. He had set up an earthly kingdom that would last for a thousand years. It was as though The Eternal was saying to mankind, *Okay, you've had thousands of years of history to run this world. Let me show you how it's done!* This kingdom included His saved ones who had risen from death, the angels, and earthly mortals. Some had come to faith during a time of great oppression. Others were born afterward. The thousand-year reign culminated in a final battle between good and evil. Sides were chosen. The Eternal ended the struggle with the words of His mouth. He then, as Creator, removed the first heavens and earth, forming their replacement. The former had no comparison to the new. This creation was beyond mortal comprehension.

A thousand years had elapsed from the new creation. The two sat together at the younger man's back patio, both enjoying a cool drink. The Savior, working in the kitchen, prepared a meal for the three of them. His redeemed friends waited for the excitement of another dinner prepared by The Hand of God. They eagerly anticipated the subsequent conversation to go along with the food, knowing it to be the more incredible nourishment. The youth-filled older one smiled at the eternally younger man saying,

"I'm glad we chose life. I had no idea it would be this good!"

Elaborate

Mattis' exploration into memory recapture was fueled by a disability few could perceive of him. He was good with the most necessary details of life going back a few years. The recall dropped off dramatically beyond that point. There were slight fuzzy visions that would be associated with familiar people though, that was about it. Curiously, these limitations had little effect on his abilities relating to his work. The problems were centered upon scenes associated with relationships. As a child, he had epilepsy brought on by a head injury. The following year after his first grand mal, his doctors prescribed a medication to control his seizures. Over time the medical profession drastically reduced the prescribed dosages of this medicine after finding it to be toxic to many who received it during the same timeframe as Mattis. The combination of the injury, the seizures, and the meds to control them had erased most of his long-term memories. Those memories were replaced by a more profound sense akin to bonding. He was keenly aware of others and his relation to them. The problem was that the details were missing.

"There, that's enough. I can almost smell the air near the lake now! I'm blown away at how fresh and tangible this is. Can you take the anterior carrier wave down three points? I think by reducing the draw, my end will sharpen. We can always go back to recording. Let's see what this will do in real-time!" Finn moved a slider down three notches on the wireless remote in his hands. The effect was immediate. Mattis' face went vacant. Drool began to flow in a long stream from the left side of his mouth in the most uncharacteristic fashion to the man and his fastidious nature.

In stark contrast to the view of the vegetated human slumped over in his chair, the experience within this man was the highest form of coherence he had ever known. Fearing he had cooked Mattis' brain, Finn quickly pushed the slider back to its home position. The interface module implanted just under Mattis' scull went dark. Like turning on a switch to Finn's eyes and turning it off on Mattis' end, the latter's countenance changed utterly as the test was paused.

"What happened?"

"It looked like you were brain dead, Mattis!" exclaimed Finn. Wiping saliva off the side of his face, Mattis replied while looking at a large spit-soaked wet patch on his belly.

"Really? That's strange. Maybe it's like an intensified dream state because I was there! We'll talk more later. Let's get back to it. Push it back slowly to where you had the counts before." Seeing the look on Finn's face, Mattis insisted, "I'm fine! Trust me, and I won't hold you accountable! If you fry my mind, I won't be able to anyway!"

"Ah, that's comforting!"

"Just do it!" Mattis insisted with a chuckle.

"Okay, okay! Sit back then but, maybe you should get some kinda bib or something."

"Just don't take any pictures or anything!" Mattis smirked. Finn engaged the control once again and slowly pushed the slider forward on the Lyapunov module's interface. Mattis' eyes went vacant, and moisture began to gather in the corner of his mouth once again.

Mattis was sitting on the slightly damp boards of the dock on his grandfather's property. The lake air was perfect with humidity that allowed a sensation to be experienced in many forms. The smell in the air and its flavor were connected to this place. The smell of the air, the taste of the lake water, and even its fish had a shared quality. His grandfather Mads had been his primary focus on trips to this place. He hadn't realized until now the elemental markers of those days.

Mattis knew this was merely a memory. The experiment he was conducting on himself with the help of his assistant Finn Markov was just that, an experiment. He was fully aware of his surroundings outside of this dreamlike state. This was beyond a hallucination, and it was difficult to understand why he could discern these two realities. It was beyond memory, more like time travel.

Mattis picked himself up off of the dock and made his way back to the house on the other side of the lake road. He walked through the freshly cut lake lot's field lined with paper birch trees. The lake air was now mixed with the chlorophyll of the lawn and a faint scent of birch bark. Next to join his experience was the dry smell of the clay and gravel road as Mattis crossed it and gave the gravel a kick. Ahead was "The Villa," a garage with a small bedroom and storage room built above it. His grandfather had always called this building by that name. It wasn't until his late teens that Mattis heard the word "Villa" in conversation when he realized the definition in his mind was wrong. By this time, his grandfather had passed away. The true meaning put a smile on his face thinking of the old man's playful sense of humor.

"The Villa" was split level, the garage meeting the lake road and built into the hill. The upper rooms of "The Villa" and adjacent house were accessible at the hilltop. Mattis walked the gradual inclined path to the top as he took in the scene. From the top of the small knoll, he looked to the south, behind "The Villa" at the chicken coup and its fenced-in yard. Fortunately, this particular day only added a faint hint of the smell of chicken husbandry. He liked his grandfather's chickens, especially the rooster, not minding its early morning crowing.

From the top of the hill, the grounds toward the front acreage of the property came into view. The half-acre vegetable garden off to the east corner amidst the sight of his grandfather's land was there like a vibrant green welcome sign. Mattis never understood his grandfather's love of toiling from the early morning until noon, manicuring this patch of ground. He did, however, enjoy its produce. The smell of the tilled soil hit his nose as he strolled down the path to find Mads on his knees pulling weeds next to a row of radishes.

Thirty blinding white flashes ensued as a conglomeration of memory combined with what happened next to Mattis'. His grandfather pulled a radish out of the ground and tossed it to him, saying,

"Here, bought time you got outta bed Matt! There's plenty more weeds here." Then added with a wry smile, "Arbeta djävlar, i graven får de vila!" Mattis caught the radish, wiped off the dirt, and bit it off from its greens. The light horseradish sensation of the vegetable, the smell of the soil and grass were overpowering. Mattis chuckled as he dropped to his knees and began to pull weeds alongside the vision of a man that he had idolized from his earliest memories.

He uprooted a weed and paused, knowing that his goal of gaining memories that were more than faint wisps of feeling was coming to fruition. The knowledge that he previously had no more substance within than the bonds that created them. This was the goal of Mattis' research into memory recapture. The dream had become a reality.

Mads had spoken of his monthly custom of bathing in the poverty of the life he had left in the old country. The unmistakable smell of his grandfather hit Mattis, light perspiration mixed with deodorant. Not at all unpleasant. It was an olfactory fingerprint. After what seemed to be an hour, Mads spoke up, saying,

"We need to go into town. We need minnows and groceries." Mattis knew what this meant. The rest of the day would be spent with his grandfather's rounds. The two made their way to the "truck," as Mads referred to his ancient 62' Dodge van. The light blue hand-painted van sat just across the property to the west. Reaching for the passenger door handle, Mattis pulled it open and jumped in, noting the strong scent of oil and gas emanating from the engine's doghouse cowl between the two front seats. Mads called, "Taffy! Come for a ride in the truck!" with his strongly accented English. The half-crazy outdoor alarm system of a dog bounded from the brush knowing his master's will would always include a ride. Taffy jumped past Mads and perched himself atop the engine cover, balancing like a surfer as the van meandered down the road over potholes and ruts. Mattis liked Taffy yet, more because of the dog's dedication to his grandfather, less of the fact of its appearance. The tail-wagger was a sight. He was covered in matts and blood-bloated ticks the size of almonds. Mattis was content to sit away from the nasty beast, leaning on the passenger door.

Their first stop was at the mobile home of Arne Grimmer. Taffy was told to stay in the "truck" as the two walked to the rickety front porch. Arne was either a close friend or a focus of Mads merciful heart. "Grimmer," as Mads called him, was a disabled diabetic who rarely left his lakefront home.

"Grimmer!" Mads called out after entering the mobile. The pungent smell of scotch and cigars wafted out the front door as they entered. Arne sat in his lounge chair smoking a Churchill with a bottle of booze next to him on the side table.

"Hey! Haven't seen you in a few." Grimmer replied as he shifted his six-foot-four frame in his recliner. Mads walked to the kitchen responding,

"I brought you some hotdogs and vegetables. There's some good lettuce, peas, and carrots this year. You need to eat something more than scotch."

"Yeah, just leave em' in the fridge Ted." Mads had allowed this nickname to replace his actual name years before to avoid confusion after leaving his homeland in eastern Europe and settling in Chicago, Illinois. While in his retirement to Minnesota during the early seventies, he allowed the moniker to follow him. Though Mattis felt a little privileged knowing his grandfather's true name, Ted was his persona here in rural Minnesota.

They made all the stops Mattis had expected, including the bait shop and The Buckhorn Bar in McGregor. It was an average hole in the wall you'd expect in the small town. The sights matched the smells within. Stale beer, cigarettes, and fried food. Mads always stopped in to say hello to his friends there, had one beer, and "shook dice." Mattis never saw him win the small challenge. He suspected it was just something fun to do. Mads would always make a big deal out of his roll. The pile of dice was thrown into the cup. He would grab it by the top, shake it wildly, slam it once on the bar top, and pour out its contents. Mads' big smile accompanied his reaction every time as he exclaimed,

"Next time, we'll get it, Matt!" Mattis knew this place was just another stop for his grandfather to make his presence known. He made sure others knew he was available. The acquaintances and friends he had made over the twenty-plus years of life he spent in this part of the country knew him for his genuine character. They relied on the old man with a strong accent from the old country. He belonged to them and they to him.

Mattis jumped into the passenger seat of the van as Mads shifted the "truck" into gear. Taffy once again began his balancing act upon the van's doghouse as they headed down the road as the sun was setting. Thirty blinding white flashes occurred once again as Mattis' eyes cleared to the patient's attention of Finn.

"Finn! I can't begin to explain the details! I don't think I experienced it that way the first time. That was more than a memory. It was like tapping into the purest HI definition reality emersion imaginable. It was like something beyond what we experience in the norm. My disability was erased. It was like a superhero power!"

"I'm just a little weirded out by what we might be adding to society, Mattis. I can see deep emersion memory cafes on every corner of town filled with drooling patrons! It'll be like the new opium den." Finn smirked.

"Yeah, I can see the requirement of wearing a helmet stuffed with absorbent mats!" Mattis replied with a chuckle

66

then, in a more serious tone, "Finn, you can't imagine how big of a help this will be. Just think how enhancing memory for the average person will affect this world. If loss of memory isn't an issue, things will be very different." Finn's wry smile faded as Mattis' words began to solidify in his mind.

"I hate to say this but, some memories are best lost, Mattis. The moral, social, and scientific implications could be immeasurable."

"Agreed but, let's put this in focus. There are abundant examples of benign things that can be used for nefarious goals. They can be used equally for good. A knife to cut your steak or someone's throat. I'm sorry but, stopping now isn't an option for me, Finn. Are you still in?"

"I'm in Mattis."

Tripe

"There's a bit of truth to that," He said while eying the Great Dane's horse-like appearance, "although I can't see this one having the guts to be a warhorse for a monkey. He's a lover, not a fighter." Ernest smiled as the idea of a monkey riding a horse into battle struck him with an inward giggle.

"That's not the idea, Ernest. It's a matter of using the primate to command the dog."

"Yeah, I get it, I get it. I just can't get serious about it, Blake. I'm trying, look, I don't mean any disrespect but, you have to admit this is not a serious sport. Monkeys riding dogs through an obstacle course, how could you not laugh?"

The monkey sat atop the large dog while scratching its neck and muttering something in monkey as it shifted on the little saddle. Just then, thirty blinding white flashes occurred as Ernest turned his attention from his eccentric friend back toward the dog and monkey. There before him stood a majestic steed with a nobleman holding its reigns. The horn sounded as the rider kicked, directing its mount through the mile-long course. The sight was a study in power matched with agility and speed. The two moved down the track, around barrels, over gates, and water traps. The flawless exercise terminated as the matched pair sped to a hard stop in front of the spectator stands. Thirty blinding white flashes strobed once again as the sight regained a semblance of reality. Ernest was stunned. He was amazed at what had just occurred before his eyes. Once again, perched atop the gargantuan canine, the monkey turned toward him and inserted a finger in its nose.

Wince

"I told you... I'm, uh... just so you don't think. I mean can't, I help it because, it might be a kinda well, you know." She stood there in the hall with great effort to try and discern what Mac was trying to say. It had already been five tedious minutes of seemingly mismatched, random, uninteresting vocalizations from him. Sonja was having a hard time with this one. She was a kind soul and worked with effort with most people to reach them at their level. Mac was becoming the test she never expected.

She had been promoted to Widgetco's Director of Greater Things a year ago and was given a team of twenty Thing Analysts within her department. Her "TANs," as she called them, were tasked with scrutinizing things and comparing them with stuff that Widgetco's competitor, Stuff-It! Co.

The office cat, Steve, sauntered between their feet and rubbed up to Mac's calf as Sonja continued.

"Mac, slow down. Count to five like we talked about last week and try again." She encouraged while inwardly suppressing the desire to scream.

"One... Two..." Sonja's relaxed countenance cracked as she cut him off,

"Mac, you can count in your head!" He stopped and stared at her for an eternal second. She knowingly waited, sensing him reach the number five.

"Okay, like I've been sayin', our things aren't like that stuff. I mean, you know... remember when the, oh never mind that, I think you already know the time when the stuff started falling downstairs. The stuff just kinda fell. It was everywhere" Mac's expression went from a precision focus to an almost savant vacancy. Sonja's attention followed his, and he was eventually left stunned once again. She was trying to figure out how this man had been hired in the first place. A daydream of being dropped into a vat of quick-drying cement flashed in her mind's eye just as thirty blinding white flashes occurred.

Sonja stared through the eyes of Steve the cat and noticed the loud purring noise emanating deep within. She looked up at the Sonja that she should have been and studied her eyes from afar. There was a catlike aloofness in the eyes of her former residence matched with a more relaxed countenance in posture. The purr stopped abruptly as she witnessed "human Sonja" turn as Mac was in a mid-confused statement and walk down the hallway wholly disengaged.

Mac was now the one to be stunned. He panicked, shocked by Sonja's behavior, starring down at his shoes, unable to handle the apparent rejection his favorite boss was displaying. Sonja was a blessing to him from the first day they were acquainted. He judged her to be incredibly patient with the awkwardness that had been a painful companion from youth. Most people he encountered had little to no time for him. He knew why; he was self-aware of his disability. He could see himself speaking fluidly with another just up to the moment he opened his mouth. At that millisecond, every alternative thought crowded his mind, many basic variants, some brilliant. There was no way to convey these struggles to another. They were his burden to bear and provided a shortcut to a solitary life.

Sonja had been different up until now. He had grown to respect her in a short amount of time as he witnessed the effort she put into what Mac knew was a challenge for her. His discernment was shattered as he watched his mentor/leader act without recognizing him as human.

Sonja's entity, present within Steve, the cat, became filled with remorse for how her body, obviously piloted by a feline mind, had caused Mac to crumple. She decided and once again allowed the purring mechanism within to fire up to full volume as she moved the cat's head toward Mac's leg again. She looked up and saw Mac begin to tear up, noticing him look around with embarrassment. Sonja let out a loud, trilled meow, catching his attention before bounding upward to him. Mac instinctively caught the cat in his arms and somehow knew the cat was comforting him.

He couldn't understand how or why the normally averagely affectionate cat was now almost annoyingly seeking his attention. Steve's purring grew louder as Mac's tears anointed its head. He held the cat close until his emotion subsided.

"Steve, you're a good boy, thankyou buddy," Mac said succinctly and quietly to the yellow tabby cat just as thirty blinding white flashes occurred.

Sonja, now back within her right vehicle, spun around quickly while figuring out what had just occurred and what to say to Mac to explain her (the cat's) behavior. The cat, now within its own skin, was shocked and confused to be within Mac's arms, gave out a loud hiss, and jumped away from him. Mac was now again bewildered, astonished to be amongst what appeared to be dreamlike randomness matching his emotions. Sonja, unable to disclose the truth for fear of losing all credibility, could think of nothing else but a lie. It felt like vomiting.

"Mac, I'm so sorry I walked off like that. I'm allergic to cats, especially that one. It's kinda weird too". She added, referencing the hiss. Thirty blinding white flashes occurred again, and Sonja's voice was replaced by a strange cross between a meow and unintelligible English. It was a bit like hearing cats howling in an alley at midnight. Mac began to question his own reality while viewing Sonja, who appeared equally astonished at what was emanating from her mouth. Just then, Steve spoke from across the room to them both.

"I cannot explain this yet; here we are. I walked in that body earlier", Steve the cat gestured to Sonja, "And well, I needed water, so I walked away. Now, I can speak as you do, and she has my language. I would rather not be involved but, there it is!

And now, I would like a bowl of canned food. The fish flavor, if you would please. Oh, and pardon me for hissing at you. I was startled and confused."

Both Mac and Sonja were locked onto the cat's every word in amazement, then turned toward each other in mutual shock. Sonja again let out a short, restrained cat howl which sent a chill up her spine just as thirty blinding white flashes filled the hallway.

Everything made sense to each member involved, and it was never mentioned from that point forward. Sonja continued to persevere in patience with the socially challenged. She continued to gain favor with her team of TANs. Her department broke records, at least those that didn't sell until all were rewarded with wage increases. Mac resumed efforts toward overcoming his impediment and, within five years, became Sonja's assistant director. Steve, the cat, continued to receive his canned fish daily and rarely hissed again.

Next

The day was approaching fast, there was an exhilaration within his spirit knowing a monumental change was in sight. The process had started with very little progress. Months elapsed until the pace began to increase after a year of discipline. Dr. Gerald Lenbock like every citizen, was born with overwhelming intellect producing honors, titles, and pedigree. There was no way to differentiate between one's neighbor in the sense of importance. A new way was soon to shift everything.

The aim of society was to shield the individual using the defense of its own value system. It dictated what was to be valued. It alone chose each individual to exalt through its sovereignty. No one had the discernment to point to where this power emanated. It was as though Jung's theories had personified themselves in the collective mind.

The fact that one was born with a mind worthy of a doctorate and need only mature physically to fill the clothes of a surgeon wasn't unusual. Infants routinely spoke after two weeks of life about the cosmological aspects of the known universe. The culture was self-absorbed with its perceived importance. A desire to look beyond the created was lost over time as the collective took hold.

In contrast to this unified thought, the change had taken root with a scant few who desired freedom from its tyranny. This sect that Dr. Lenbock had joined two years prior had proven to be a Godsend. They had given him access to an ancient knowledge lost to the masses that guaranteed freedom. The doctor had poured his life into the study of these documents finding life with every page received. Today, he would make his choice official. His personal records would be wiped clean.

The office building before him was similar to the others in this sector of the city. Curiously, it was sanctioned by the government as a legitimate tool of the system. Citizens were allowed the freedom to their own records to be modified as they saw fit within the confines of law. It made no difference how an official with an opposing opinion viewed the sect's ways. They were allowed to structure their lives as they wished. This by no means shielded the sect from society's mockery. He walked through the front door determined to receive the fruition of his labors.

"Next!" came the call of the clerk behind the counter. She wore a genuine smile, illuminating her countenance as a visible window to her soul. The doctor recognized her from one of the sect gatherings he had come to enjoy. He smiled back at her in mutual friendship and replied,

"I guess it's me!"

"Dr, Gerald Lenbock?" The clerk responded.

"For now, it is, Janice."

"Okay, sign here, here and here and we can make it official." Janice instructed.

The doctor signed his name on the third and final line on the boilerplate form. Thirty blinding white flashes occurred as Janice simultaneously stamped the form with the imprint *RECIEVED*. Gerald now stood before Janice stripped of all burden. All titles were removed, it was exhilarating. The expectation to impress was no longer needed. He felt naked and unashamed. The ceremony of sorts made official the transfer of honor given from society to someone greater.

Gerald knew no less than before. It was as though his ownership was transferred that day. He was now excited for what   came   next.

Element

Innumerable microscopic crystalline structures fell upwards toward the lights placed high above in the arched ceiling of the railway station. It was just past midnight. The eleven-fifteen train and those disembarking its bowels had vacated the building at least fifteen minutes ago. The station master who had been completing his tasks for the night was the sole inhabitant of the compound.

The alien substance, still under the influence of its native world and quantum placement, moved with the gravity of that place. That place was one hundred and eighty degrees out of phase with earth. With this in mind, falling upwards was anything but supernatural.

The station master continued his rubber-stamping of the hourly time-keeping documents for the railway, counted ticket sales, and prepared the deposit. The bi-weekly pickup from the six-fifteen train was rarely late, and he was in the habit of not leaving this job to the morning station master. Coffee played a significant role in the morning, and the boiler was never very reliable. It was a better idea to just complete the job at the end of his shift. It made sleep much more enjoyable.

He banded his last roll of pound notes and stuffed them into the bag filled with coin rolls and various other paper denominations. That is when the iron-like groan of bending steel came to his ears from high above, outside his station master's outbuilding in the hall, above the tracks. He quickly fastened the padlock on the drop-bag and rushed through the door to locate the source of the disturbance.

At the top of the arch, the massive iron light fixture's mount could be seen to slowly bend earthward. The groaning

77

continued as the wrought iron structure bent under the weight of the now visible microscopic deposit upon it. Curiously, at the point where the two dimensions met, one with gravity in polar opposite to the other, the effect was apparent in the rail station only. The elements continued their upward descent upon the light until the two-hundred-pound ornament broke free, pulling with it a three-foot section of the roof as it fell. Just then, thirty blinding white flashes occurred.

The scene changed before the station master's eyes. He was physically inverted and now falling from a height of one hundred and twenty feet above the ground below himself. The snap change in orientation knocked his equilibrium out of phase with his reasoning to the point that he perceived himself falling upwards. The ground below was rapidly approaching and appeared to be a kind of cloud formation. He was now at roughly fifty feet from impact when his bearings returned as the crystals aligned within his inner ears. The experience first caused a bewildered, exciting fascination, thinking himself the first human to attain unassisted flight. It seemed for that flash of time that he had perished and was ascending to glory. Now that the truth of this realm had descended upon him as he progressed his descent, terror instantly filled his heart. The pinkish cloud-like stuff was approaching quickly now after reaching terminal velocity.

The station master's body position was at a perfect right angle to the ground. This made it necessary for him to lean his head backward to view his target. It dawned on him this position would likely snap his neck like a fresh asparagus stem upon impact. His unwelcome goal was now ten feet away. Time was now moving so slowly from his perspective that he seemed to be able to count to twenty as each of his heartbeats completed its pulse of blood-filled pressure.

The station master's face entered the cotton-candy-colored material in his path downward. The resistance was slight, as if it were possible to experience diving into the water with less resistance. The unknown element was all around him now, as close as a membrane, and its resistance began to slowly increase as his fall continued. The view from within was a dreamlike experience akin to viewing warm morning sunlight through thin pinkish bedsheets. He continued to fall. His descent continued to slow until, all at once, he stopped within the stuff.

Just then, he heard the conductor yell out, *All aboard!* Immediately thirty blinding white flashes occurred. He was once again within his station master's office. Wiping the drool from his lips and sleep from his eyes, he arose to look out at the train as it left the station. He rubbed his head and said to himself, *no more late-night sausage and cucumber sandwiches for you, Jasper!* As his name whispered past his lips, the brake van car of the train passed by, allowing him to view the station's lamp fixture laying on the next set of tracks away from   him.

Failure

"How do expect me to react! I can't believe you did this again. You're an idiot, a fool. Do think you could've hidden it from everyone as long as you have without someone calling you out? What a loser."

The words fell on him like lead. Not the comforting effect of a weighted blanket, the body of a lover, or a full plate of food in the hand of a starving man but, the antithesis. This pressure was the kind that crushes the spirit. Its weight upon one's chest leaves little room to draw breath. Akin to gasping for emotional oxygen within a tank of carbon dioxide. To make things worse the words continued,

"You've proven to me that you will never attain the level you thought you would reach. I remember hearing you spill out your heart to me when you started. I told you back then you would have to work harder than everyone else. I warned you, remember? I went over all the obstacles in your way. I was shocked when you decided to go through with it anyway. You know what this does don't you? It embarrasses us!"

This new monologue poured cement into his soul. It was all true. Shame began to blanket the already stifling pressure upon him. He thought of those in his past. Ghosts of school years past slowly paraded by him. Their mocking presence distracting from the present situation, crippling depression began to inject its warm fingers into him with a physical manifestation that was equally painful as well as numbing. It was like a drug. He remembered retreating into this darkness as a way to deal with his inabilities. Unable connect with most of the kids he grew up with, he viewed most of them as beyond him. Finding it difficult to carry on a simple conversation, the words wouldn't leave his lips correctly. His mind crowded with negative thoughts refused to interact with ease. As the school years increased, he allowed the darkness to cover him, thinking it a shield from those eyes. Eyes that purposely avoided his, seeing his exterior only. He met those eyes with shame, wishing to connect yet, knowing his prison.

His only companion continued this council from as far back as he could remember. This friend learned his craft from a select few from the childhood they shared. It was a highly dysfunctional companionship but, he knew no alternative.

This "friend" witnessed the neglect filled relationship he had with his father. A man with a very different personality from his son and unable to relate. Neither shared each other's interests. Unfortunately for the young boy, he was neglected. When not ignored, his flaws were pointed out by the father. This was the only verbal interaction between the two and the "friend" learned his craft.

Over time the "friend" learned more ways to motive him. This companion would often transition between shame and arrogance. When he found a skill or physical attribute that could be admired, this messenger would use it to the extreme and persuade him to view himself as above others. It was another covering of darkness and a defense mechanism he used to shield himself from the fear of man.

As he became a young man, he began to realize his relationship with his closest friend was toxic. It was difficult to admit that this lifelong companion was bad for him. He decided to look for another friend. Someone who could tell him the truth in a way that brought light into his life. His search was fruitless with everyone he met. While there were many wonderful people in his path, they couldn't help him in the way he needed it most.

It wasn't until he picked up a book and read about someone who literally laid his life down for him that his search for that friend was over. That realization was met with thirty blinding white flashes and his life was forever changed. He came to understand his own efforts weren't enough to make him complete. This man who laid his life down was the only way to fill that need. The man said in the book he would send his friend to meet him and speak truth to him forever. That friend showed up that very day and echoed everything the book spoke of in a way that applied to him personally.

Now, things were different but, he always had visits from the old "friend" from time to time. His truth speaking friend told him this would happen and that he needed to choose which voice he would listen to. It became a new struggle, a war of thought, spirit, and will. It seemed when he doubted the truth, his old friend showed up. The doubts always fueled a desire for something he knew was bad for him yet would have temporary pleasure. The battles would continue throughout his life. The victories were won when he remembered it was his friend that paid the price that would win all his battles. He only needed to believe the truth that the job was completed already. His failures were paid for.

It boiled down to motivation. He realized his efforts combined with The Savior's finished work always had a victorious outcome if it fit with the will of his best friend.

"I think you'd better leave. I've told you before, I'm not listening to you anymore. I won't argue, you're right about me but, it's not about me anymore. I don't need to struggle to satisfy you or anybody else either! Your words have never helped anyway. Get out!"

Peace once again came to him like a whisper. He resolved to try again, knowing it was the path he was being led toward. The pressure to perform could now be ignored as he remembered   Truth.

A Grand Time

Jasin walked into the house to grab an iced tea. The last customer had left the front yard estate sale as she counted and pocketed the proceeds while walking to the refrigerator. Oddly, she was detoured to the hallway. A sweet smell emanated from the attic having the aroma of perfectly ripened raspberries, caramel, and bananas. The scent wasn't at all unpleasant, just strange. Strong enough to evoke an uncanny fear within Jasin. She couldn't remember putting anything in the attic that could rot and wondered why the smell was so potent without smelling off. She and her husband Fred had recently signed the papers, receiving the home as an inheritance from her recently departed grandmother Jas-Anne. It was at least a year now that Jas-Anne had been moved to a nursing home.

Jas-Anne had been an active woman all her life, so, as expected, it was a difficult decision for the family to persuade her to enter the care center. She was a fit, healthy, beautiful woman of ninety-three when her health made a turn toward those of her age group. Medical science had progressed exponentially over the last few decades in a similar multiplied gain increase that all sciences had enjoyed over the previous hundred years. Unfortunately, even in 2066, medicine had failed to touch her ailments sufficiently to stave off the terminal diagnosis she received six months before her death.

Jasin was her grandmother's favorite. It wasn't because she was named after her. She and Jasin Anne Freedom just clicked. It was never discussed, and the old woman would have denied it. All twelve of her grandchildren and great-grandchildren never would have suspected it anyway. This truth was sealed away in the matriarch's heart. Jasin knew it was unspoken, an almost spiritual connection with her grandmother. This explained the harshness of the sudden loss of a critical foundation in her life.

Jasin walked to the hallway between the bedrooms and the front room and stared up at the attic's entry. The rectangular white paneled door monolithically hung in its place as the smell protruded from it with greater intensity. She reached up and pulled the rope firmly, watching as the door swung out of the way, revealing the folded ladder attached. A second pull rope was grasped, and the ladder descended to the floor. Jasin pushed in the latch to lock it in place and, without a second thought, began to ascend the steps. The ten-foot ceilings made her travel slightly prolonged, and with each progression came a more pronounced effect upon her olfactory senses. The raspberry, caramel, and banana were now replaced with chocolate, vanilla, and hot bread as she reached the landing. It was pitched black inside the roof even at this noon hour so, she reached for the familiar light switch. This same switch greeted her during her younger years when grandma allowed her to explore the attic independently. It was a distant land full of memory and treasure. Jas-Anne made sure to leave an oriental rug and a few chests filled with pictures and relics from the past in the corner, knowing Jasin would be drawn to their secrets. She would make sure to add new findings within reach before her granddaughter's subsequent visits.

The light switch, when turned on, unexpectedly produced thirty blinding white flashes, and Jasin was now in a bakery she had never seen until now. The shock began to register after this abrupt change in surroundings. The humid heat of home was replaced by a chill in the air. She looked out the window to see snow lightly falling. The cold entered her heart and mind with fear. She began to shake uncontrollably, her mind grasping possibilities and attempting a logic that eluded her.

"*Get ahold of yourself, Jasin!*" She spoke out loud, without thinking first. She stopped and looked around, and for some reason, nobody took any notice of her. Jasin's immediate perceptions were now overtaken with sense as she began to wonder how and why she was here, a world away from Covington, Louisiana. Was she dreaming, or was this reality? Jasin decided to test the waters and bumped into a giant man next to her in the pastry line. The old man dressed in what appeared to be fisherman's clothes turned toward his shoulder and rubbed it with a confused look on his face. He turned his head back toward the barista behind the counter, now with a renewed desire for his morning coffee and bocconotto. She spoke out loud, "Hello, can anyone hear me? I'm right here!" She was quiet at first, then gradually louder while seeing no response in any patrons in the queue within the shop.

She began to wonder what the purpose of this place was to her. Was it imagination, had she died and was now wandering as a ghost, was it some kind of spiritual vision, was she having a seizure and this vision was linked, or could the smells she experienced while in the real world have been some kind of drug? There were no answers to these questions in this place.

She turned, leaving the shop, looking up and down the street in a panic for anything with reference to reality. The shops lining the street were quaint, natural establishments, each having an old-world feel and all signage in Italian. She rushed past a butcher, fishmonger's, a candy shop, and a bookstore before coming to its attached newsstand. At the top of the town's local paper, she found the date above a myriad of Italian words covering the page in various sizes of type, all unintelligible from her perspective. The year in print 1995, the same year her grandmother had spent in Italy. But was this the same town? She still had no idea where she was so, that didn't matter much anyway. The recollection of her grandmother's stories was limited. She only knew that it was a town on the southern coast of Italy. Come to think of it, Jas-Anne spoke very little of this year abroad. It made Jasin even more curious as to why she saw this vision.

While unsure of what else to do, she had an uncanny pull within her to wander back to the little bakery. It was almost the same draw that the smells emanating from the attic door aroused in her. She was lost, confused, untethered, and afraid yet, there seemed to be a feeling of comfort associated with the bakery. She reached the door and looked up to read the sign, Pasticceria Panza, next to the doorway. The smells once again hit her nose as she entered the shop. The aromas matched what she had experienced at home, but, now, due to context, they were muted. Looking around again, she viewed the cases filled with freshly baked bread, pastries, cookies, and confections that equaled the deliciousness of their smells visually. The line in front of the counter was down to two people. Figuring her previous invisibility, she wandered aimlessly throughout the shop, unsure what to do next. Jasin sneezed, and to her surprise, an elderly lady turned and said,

"Salute!" Jasin was now even more confused and answered in English,

"Thank you." The lady smiled and turned back toward the counter.

Ahead of this woman was a young lady about her height, build, and hair color. The woman spoke her order to the lady behind the counter in perfect Italian with an American accent undetected by Jasin. With pastries and coffee in hand, she turned and walked out the door as Jasin looked the other way. The older lady with coffee in hand once again smiled at her on her way outside as well.

Jasin, still feeling out of sorts, walked up to the counter and sheepishly said,

"Hello, do you speak English?" The lady behind the counter smiled and said,

"Torno così presto? Hai dimenticato qualcosa?" translated, "Back so soon? Did you forget something?" She looked slightly confused and said, "Mi dispiace non parlo inglese." Translated,

"I'm sorry, I don't speak English." The woman smiled and continued in Italian, "Parli un Italiano così bello, hai finito le parole? A proposito, come hai fatto a cambiarti i vestiti così in *fretta?* Translated, "You speak such beautiful Italian, did you run out of words? By the way, how did you change your clothes so fast?" Jasin looked confused, decided to sit down for a while. Knowing she might be asked to leave if she didn't buy something, she reverted to pointing to a pastry and coffee. The woman behind the counter, unsure what was going on, decided not to be offended and pulled the goods from the display case. Jasin handed her ten dollars and turned to walk to a nearby table. The lady rushed after her, exclaiming,

"Sono troppi soldi, signorina!" Translated, "This is too much money, miss!" Jasin, unsure what to do, pulled out another ten dollars, at which the woman held up her hand to prevent it. Jasin, now understanding, put it back in her pocket, smiled and held up her hand, pointed to the woman, and said,

"No, it's for you, please take it!" The lady blushed and smiled herself, nodded her head, and walked back to the till. Jasin began eating her treats and drinking the best coffee of her life. It was the medicine needed to calm her. She finished the last bit of pastry when the young woman in front of her in line earlier walked back inside the bakery. This time Jasin was able to see her face. It was like looking into a mirror for the first time. The woman glanced toward Jasin and did a double-take. Stumbling with distraction, she raced to the counter. She then asked for a refill in perfect Italian. The lady behind the counter chuckled, now knowing her mistake of confusing her with Jasin. The two of them spoke, and the clerk pointed at Jasin a few times and smiled. The woman excused herself and turned again toward the door.

"Wait! Please, can I speak to you for a moment?" The woman stopped and awkwardly approached Jasin's table. "Do you speak English?" The woman slowly replied,

"Yes, I do."

"I'm so sorry. I couldn't help but see that you look like we could be related. I could see the lady behind the counter must have confused us too. I know you don't know me but, I'm lost and need help." Jasin stopped and looked down at the table with shame, thinking she had said too much. To her surprise, she felt a hand on her own and looked up with tears in her eyes. Her eyes were met with a familiar look from the eyes of the woman she knew was more than a stranger. Jasin, filled with wonder, looked into the eyes of this young woman, knowing a connection had been made with minimal effort. The lady smiled and said,

"Honey, come with me. We can talk." The two then left the bakery. As they walked, several feral cats raced past them in one of the alleys on their way to the woman's home. Jasin followed the woman to a beautiful, old three-story apartment in the center of town. They climbed the stairs to her top-floor apartment. After walking through the door, Jasin once again began to perceive familiar smells. There were hints of similar fragrances that had drawn her up the attic stairs earlier that day. This experience added to the calming effect she began to experience after returning to the bakery and meeting this lady. Jasin had her suspicions about who this woman was, but it seemed much too fantastic to be true. She decided to ride it out and see where the experience would lead.

Jasin sat on the couch as the woman put on some water to boil and brought out her tea service tray. Jasin once again kept her mouth shut with wonder as she began to inventory the woman's belongings, starting with the tea service tray. The random familiar items scattered in various locations, shelves, and tabletops all had one thing in common. Every one of them had been held back from the estate sale for Jasin's personal collection. They were exact replicas yet, much newer and lacking the faded charm that gave them the character Jasin deemed nostalgic to her grandmother Jas-Anne. Just then, the tea kettle began to scream from the kitchen before the woman turned it off and returned to her guest.

She poured the hot water into the teapot and walked back to return it to the kitchen before sitting down in the chair next to the couch.

"So, let's start slow. What's your name, and where are you from, Honey?"

Jasin's eyes were remiss at hiding her anticipation of the woman's question. She slowly responded, knowing her host could react in a myriad of ways.

"My name is Jasin Anne Freedom. I'm from Covington, Louisiana." The woman was visibly shocked even more than her stumble within the bakery upon seeing Jasin for the first time. There was an awkward silence that filled the one-bedroom flat. The woman picked up the teapot and began pouring tea, stopping halfway through the second cup and said,

"Honey, do expect me to believe that? I mean, you're my age. I've never seen you before either. How could you be from my hometown? I would know you! You would've gone to my high school, known all the same people. Is this a joke?" Jasin, now treading lightly, added,

"I know this seems crazy but, I should tell you how this began. I was at home a few hours ago. I noticed smells coming from my attic, and when I climbed the stairs and turned on the light, I was transported to that bakery. The smells matched. If this isn't crazy enough for you, I was born in 2044. The woman sat with her mouth open, half in amazement, half in suspicion, transfixed to her every word.

Jasin watched her knowing the wheels in her head were spinning so, she allowed her to process the unbelievable. The woman's complexion turned pale.

"If you didn't look like me, I wouldn't be sitting here now. The thing is, I can't seem to wake up from this dream."

"I've never had a dream with someone in it thinking they were dreaming. If this is a dream, it's the clearest one I've had." Jasin responded with a note of fear in her own voice. Her mind was racing when she remembered something that would anchor her words to the truth.

"This might help you believe me." She added gently, knowing the woman was reeling in this conflict to reality. Jasin reached into her pocket and pulled out her cell phone. She knew they were in use in the nineties yet, they were nothing like the instrument she displayed. Jasin accessed a file on the screen then, the device projected a high-definition 3D image above it of her hometown. Jasin had taken these pictures last week during a birthday party. She just happened to have taken some shots of the preparation for the party that featured various sites around town.

The woman broke. The stunned look on her face was amplified yet, now she believed Jasin's testimony.

"How could-, I don't under-. What could-." She mumbled while staring in amazement at the image floating above the phone. Jasin, now with a partner to share her confusion, replied,

"I don't know. I wish I did. Are we some kind of time-dimensional version of the same person? I mean, you look like you could be my sister. We're not exactly alike, but?"

"Jasin, my name is Jas-Anne Freedom. Do you know that name?" Jasin's strangest suspicion was confirmed as she was equally excited and apprehensive of the truth.

"You are my grandmother! I really don't know what this means. I'm not really sure what to call you now that I see you as my age."

"Grandmother! Grandma Jas-Anne! When is this gonna end! So, I guess If I'm your grandma, there must be a grandpa, right?" At once, a strange feeling came over both of them, and miraculously, they understood, specific questions might be off-limits. "Oh, never mind, we might mess up the excitement of finding him myself. I can't get over the idea that I'll live life to that age. Will I be a good grandma Jasin?"

"You are the best. You're more like my best friend." Jasin thought it best not to mention her passing at this time. "I was always able to come to you when we both needed a laugh, and you've always been there for me to help me talk out my problems.

"This is awkward, Jasin. You know me better than I know myself. I'm sorry but, I've just met you."

"Well, I guess I'll have the same experience eventually. Once this goes back to normal, you'll watch me grown up from a newborn. That's kinda similar right?"

"I see what you mean. Babies aren't aware of who they are with until much later. So, let's figure this out. Why do you think we're meeting like this?"

"Not sure but, I guess I've never really been able to place myself at your age. Now that I think about it seeing you here has really given me confidence in my own future. I mean, you made it through life with a lot to be proud of!" Jasin, once again felt caution to disclose anymore, simply smiled with the same warmth she usually would have toward her grandmother at an older age. It was uncanny how this paradigm was beginning to change her perspective on people in general. She was starting to see humanity in all of its asymmetrical generations in a way that seemed to gather them together in a uniform line. Jas-Anne simultaneously had a similar thought.

The two young ladies spent their remaining daylight hours discussing this topic as the night crept through the windows. A chill ran through the air, and Jas-Anne decided to make a fire in the woodstove just as dusk settled in.

"Well, we should probably get you settled in for the night," Jas-Anne declared just before switching on the light switch. With a flip of the switch, there occurred thirty blinding white flashes occurred, and every trace of Jasin Anne Freedom was gone. Jas-Anne stood staring at the spot where her granddaughter had sat, once again in shock.

Jas-Anne left Italy later that same month for home. She realized that she had been changed, whether her experience was a vision, hallucination, or mental illness. Gone was her need to find a life away from home. It was apparent to her from that point onward that her life was not her own. She was a part of something greater.

Later in life, Jas-Anne's daughter-in-law gave birth to a baby girl. The newborn's parents, without consulting Jas-Anne, decided to name the baby Jasin Anne Freedom. Jas-Anne broke down and cried with joy as the culmination of experiences from her youth were confirmed physically. She was now able to watch this child who would become her best friend grow up to be the woman she knew she would become.

The Desk

"The storm's coming."

He said while looking out at the frost on the lawn outside the kitchen window,

"Do you know where I put my plaid scarf? Betcha this storm's gonna hit early tonight."

"I hope so! I love a good blizzard!" Frank's wife Kate replied, "When I was a kid, Mom, Dad, and I would wait for the biggest storm of the year to run outside in our swimsuits."

"Why the hell would you do that?" Frank hated the winter, the cold, the sweaters. It was a violin of death to him. Lifelessness reigned the struggle of nature's tormented victims, the steel skies, the frozen air. It was a time to be endured, not celebrated. At least that's what he tried to remind himself.

"It was so fun! We ran outside into the snowdrifts and forced ourselves to make snow angels! The first one back into the house was the loser. They had to make the cocoa, a fire in the woodstove, and pull out the blankets for everyone else!"

"So, who did all that?"

"Mom usually lost. I kinda think she did on purpose most of the time. Dad never did. There was one time while he was still young. I must've been ten. He stayed out too long and got frostbite. I guess it was pretty stupid but, that's probably where I got my competitive edge."

"Frostbite!" Frank's original opinion of the season bolstered, "You guys were nuts! So, was he okay?"

"Yeah, well, he only lost two toes."

"What the hell, are you serious?"

"No, I'm joking! He had to have some dead skin removed but, he never lost any appendages!"

"Well, you're not helping to change my mind on the cold."

"I know but, the warm inside stuff is nice, right?"

"Yeah, I guess, but a warm beach sounds better."

The cold front did indeed arrive early as the couple sat inside the cabin atop a ridge deep within the Blue Mountains of Eastern Washington State. It was Kate's family's place; she was the youngest of three siblings and the only one interested in using the land. Her parents had passed away in an automobile accident when she was in her early twenties. This was her memorial week for them.

The forecast for the week turned out to be a disappointment to Frank, affecting Kate in the exact opposite way. It called for sub-zero temperatures that would plummet deeper with the wind-chill effect. There was even a chance a blizzard might find its way to the lonely ridgetop residence. The cabin was ten miles from the nearest town if you could draw a line on the map to it. In terms of travel, it would take at least forty minutes on the switchback dirt roads that traversed the ridges. These estimates were for good weather conditions to reach it.

"I think we should make a run to Dayton before that blizzard shows up. Are you game?" Frank asked, hoping to buy some snacks and a couple of ribeyes. If he was going to be stuck inside, he might as well have his favorite grub.

"That sounds like a great idea. If we go now, we might get there before all the good stuff's been cleaned out! Just let me get a list together first." She pulled out a notepad from the old desk that was passed down through the generations of her family. She really had no idea how far back the antique's history traveled. The desktop seemed to bind as she lowered it. She raised it again and looked to see something was, in fact jamming the lid's way. It was a piece of leather protruding from what appeared to be a kind of notch inside the desk. She had never noticed it before, and it gave her goosebumps for some unknown reason.

"Look at this, Frank. Have you ever seen this?" She tugged on the leather without successfully freeing it. "I can't pull it out. Can you?" Frank walked to the desk and got down on his knees to get a closer look inside. He grabbed the leather strap and gave it a tug noticing what appeared to be a panel moving slightly with each jerk.

"I'm not sure, but this looks like one of those security desks. I remember seeing a documentary a few years back. I think it was on the White House. I could be wrong, anyway. I think it was a desk in the Oval Office that had secret compartments in it. You had to move the correct triggers to get the panel to open up. This might be built similarly. Who knows, maybe you'll find Blackbeard's treasure map inside this old thing!" He gave Kate a playful smirk and stood back up.

"You really think it could be built that way? How fun! Well, we better not try to figure it out now and get stuck on the road with a treasure map! We could freeze to death before finding our booty!" She replied.

"Aaarrrggg Captain! Let's not shiver me timbers!"

"Come on, you scallywag! Go warm up the pickup."

"Good idea, I'll be outside." Frank turned toward the door and grabbed his coat, hat, wallet, and keys before pulling the door open to the icy cold that pushed against the warmth within the cabin as he left.

Kate finished her list and grabbed her belongings as well. The cold once again intruded into the room as the door closed behind her. The old Ford pickup sat in front of the cabin, chugging away as the engine warmed to operating temperature. Not warmed enough to allow the heat to flow, the two sat on the bench seat, not quite shivering. Frank admitted to himself that the cold on this bright morning was refreshing. His anticipation of the truck's heat was almost an event-like desire. Kate slid closer to him just before the truck's engine smoothed to a staggering purr. She switched on the heat as Frank moved the shifter to drive.

The truck creaked down the steep dirt switchback before the next turn, almost a hairpin. The second downhill run insight also revealed tiny dust-like snowflakes beginning to fall lightly all around them.

"Well, hope we can get there and back before it gets worse." He pushed his foot into the accelerator a bit more as the worn work truck obeyed like an old nag down the road. Three more switchbacks ensued before the snow stopped, the clouds broke again, allowing the sun to shine on a powder sugar-coated mountain scene all around them. The journey took them out of the mountain switchbacks into wheat stalk stubble rolling hills equally dusted with snow. It was beautiful.

The remaining drive to town was a peacefully bumpy trip through the freshly transformed winter landscape. The grocery store visit being uneventful. The two loaded the pickup and started the return trip home just as light snow began to fall once again. As the cold white substance increased its descent, Frank began to worry as the pickup left the rolling hills and started the trek up the first switchback. The old vehicle lost traction a few times on the way, and Frank pulled over.

"I'm gonna lock the hubs. It's not worth wrecking and having to carry groceries to the cabin." Kate simply smiled as he jumped out of the cab. Finishing the job, he jumped back in and engaged the four-wheel-drive lever. The ancient machine grunted and started pulling with power up the hill toward the first switchback. The snowfall increased with each new switchback climb. Upon reaching the cabin, six new inches were already on the ground.

The couple gathered the groceries and filled the kitchen counter with them before slamming the cabin door. The cold once again was defeated as the two huddled near the woodstove to warm up. Now both warmed up and the groceries put away, they stopped, looked at each other, and said simultaneously,

"The desk!" Both turned toward the relic, and an eerie sense of reverence came over them. Thoughts of Geraldo Rivera opening Al Capone's vault were quickly suppressed within their minds though, they hadn't discussed that possible similarity out loud.

"Where should we start?" Kate blurted out after both stood in front of the antique. They were speechless for at least a minute while in thought.

"Well, the one in that documentary had like three or four triggers. You had to operate them in the right sequence before the compartment would open."

"Well, let's clear it out then first!" She exclaimed excitedly. Frank grabbed the empty box from the grocery load, and they began pulling out the desk's contents. With each batch of papers and knickknacks removed, something caught Kate's eye that slowed down the process. Not an unwelcomed delay from either's perspective, the sentimental items cut loose a flood of wonder, a new insight, or a shared memory to each.

"Wow, look at this! I didn't realize my dad worked as a logger. I remember my mom teasing him once in a while about his snoring and something to do with taking away his saw. I never knew there was a back story." Frank held up a photo from twenty years ago" Remember this day? The picture was of the two of them still in high school in an old Chevy Vega.

"Oh my gosh! The Yellow Turd! I hated that car until I loved it! Kate giggled.

" Ya just needed the right guy with a V-8 handy." Frank said with a wink. "That was the definition of a sleeper. Nobody expected that car to move like it did. Did I ever tell you when I borrowed it from you and a guy-." Frank stopped, thinking better of telling the story.

"What, this is news to me! You've already busted yourself. You better finish your story, Bub!" She shot back at him with mock fury in her eyes.

"Well, I borrowed it one night and had to grab something from my dad's shop on Alameda one night around eight o'clock. I was at a stop sign, and this guy pulled up next to me in a Porsche Carrera. He looked like a rich snob, so, as a joke, I tapped my horn and pointed forward. He laughed at the dumb kid in the beater Vega but hit it hard when the light turned green. I didn't think he would take the challenge so, I wasn't ready. He was about four car lengths away before I dropped the clutch and spun the wheels a little too much. He was about a quarter of the way to the next light by the time I was able to get traction. I think he saw me gaining on him behind because I could tell he hit the gas again hard just as I passed him. He lost control, jumped the curb, and side-swiped a fire hydrant before pulling it back on the road. I made it to the next red light, then made a "u" turn to check on him. He was on the side of the road looking at the right side of the car when I got there."

"Was he mad at you?"

"Na, I didn't do anything to him. He was pretty upset at himself and interested in your car. Seemed like a nice guy. I felt pretty bad about it. That was the end of my drag racing days!"

"That's funny! I never told you I had a few races of my own so, I know what you mean. It was fun to see the expression on the faces of the guys with their Camaros and Mustangs. The Turd was ugly but, it had the runs!" She smirked

"That's nasty!" The stories fueled by various items from the desk continued until dusk as the remaining items were boxed. Frank grabbed the table, and with Kate's help, they both turned it upside down. For fifteen minutes, they felt around the underside, legs, and sides of the furniture until Kate noticed a small decorative scroll similar to twenty or more of the same on the bottom face of the desk. It had an air gap around it like a button. She pushed it without being able to get it to move.

"Maybe it needs to be right-side-up for the mechanism to move," Frank said and began to pick it up again. Kate helped, and they set the heavy piece back on its legs. Frank gestured at the trigger, saying,

"It's all you." Kate pushed the button again, after which an audible pop was heard, and the top decorative molding of the left-hand leg popped out, revealing a small hidden drawer.

"Wow, look at that!" Kate squealed and fully opened the compartment. There inside the drawer, a ring with a small diamond and a tiny key was taped. Kate pulled out the ring and key and examined them both. Having worked at a jewelry store in the past, she knew what to look for.

"I really need my loupe but, it looks pretty good. Probably at least a quarter carat. Pretty cool but, this key is more interesting." She pocketed the items and looked closer at the inside of the drawer.

"Look, Frank. Does that look normal?"
He got down on his knees and peered inside the opening, seeing what Kate pointed out. There seemed to be a latch with a spring holding the drawer from coming all the way out. He reached in halfway, unable to get at the latch with his large hand, and said,

"I can't reach it. You try." As he pulled out his hand. Kate reached in with some effort and released the latch. The drawer came out another quarter inch and stopped while another linkage sound within the desk clicked. She pulled her hand out completely, and the drawer hung onto the desk with a slight angle. Frank grabbed it and lifted it slightly, and it was able to be pulled free. A small envelope dropped to the floor as the drawer was removed. Kate picked it up and read aloud the handwritten note within,

"*June 23, 1913, Dear Captain Abner Oaks, I've pondered the claims you have made regarding time travel, The Collective, The Deluge, and the KSP particles you claim exist throughout the known universe. I appreciate the time you have taken to document these fascinating theories, and I will make a serious effort to study them. Yours truly, Erwin Schrödinger.* Wow, that's amazing! I had no Idea my great-great-grandfather Abner was a captain or in contact with someone like Schrödinger. I wonder what this means?" Kate's eyes went vacant as she daydreamed the implications of the note.

"I can't see anything in this old thing being any more valuable than that but, lemme see that key. Kate, still in a daze, reached into her pocket and handed him the key. Peering into the drawer's recess, he was able to see a keyhole a quarter of the way inside pointing at a right angle. Once again, unable to reach inside sufficiently, he handed the key back to Kate, saying,

"You try. My mitts don't fit." Kate snapped out of her thoughts and, with some effort, positioned her hand inside the recess, managing to insert the key after dropping it twice. She stopped and looked at Frank, saying,

"Well, here it goes." Once again, she tried but was unable to turn the tumbler. Frank motioned to the drawer, and she pulled it open with her other hand. Once again, she pushed the lock, and it turned, allowing the central drawer to come out all the way. Like the last drawer, it hung at a slight angle, not quite able to be removed. Kate picked it up slightly and pulled it as another metallic linkage clicked and the opposite top leg ornament popped open. Inside this small drawer was a glass vial held tight by a brass clamp to the inside of the drawer's bottom. She entirely removed the drawer in the same manner as the others and peered into the seemingly empty glass container.

"It looks empty, humph." Discouraged, she decided to bring it in closer to the light. Then she saw the diamond-like shimmer for a flash with the correct angle. "Look at this. I thought it was empty but, there's something in there. See, you gotta catch the light just right!" Frank gently took ahold of the canister and turned in his hands while looking into it intently.

"Woah, that's a trip. The way it catches the light is so weird. I can't even see what's in there until the light hits it. It's blinding. What is it? I mean, I'm a little freaked out, Kate." He handed the small container back to her even more carefully. If this is related to that note, well, I think we might want to just put it back and forget about it." Kate received the vial with equal care and stepped backward, tripping over the last drawer that was removed. The drawer shot forward as her foot lost traction. She attempted to regain her footing before becoming off-balanced once again. She fell hard on her left side as Frank lunged toward the vial to steady it. He managed to grab it out of the air after she lost her grip. Then it was his turn to fumble. He started out looking like a wide receiver but, his trajectory toward the leading edge of an open door turned a victorious attempt into a cruel comedy. He collided with the door at his right shoulder, and once again, the sealed glass tube was aloft. They were now trapped in what seemed like a slow-motion film. They could only watch it fly from his hand into the kitchen. I shattered against the granite countertop. Frank sat up, groaned and rubbed his shoulder, and said,

"Well, that didn't go like I thought it would. I guess it wasn't a big deal. After all, might be just glitter or something. You okay?"

"Yeah, just a little upset. If that thing was special, we'd never know now. By the way, that was epic!" She smiled genuinely and picked herself up. The two hobbled into the kitchen to survey the debris. The glass was contained to about a quarter of the small kitchen in tiny shards.

"Do we even have a dustpan up here? Frank inquired.

"Come on, you know me!" Kate pulled out a broom and dustpan from the closet and started sweeping. The clean-up was quick, and the shards were thrown into the garbage can, soon to be taken to the landfill.

The two put the desk back together and refilled it. Once finishing, the two paused and looked into each other's eyes, smiled, and shrugged. Kate spoke first to break the silence.

"Well, at least we have these," she said, holding up the ring and the small envelope. "They're pretty amazing."

"Might even be worth something."

"I don't think I would part with this note. Who knows what the significance of the ring has. If they've been hidden here this long, they might both be important. Well, dinner, it's getting late." Kate turned to the kitchen once again with Frank in toe. The two opened cans of chili and joined them with hotdogs.

They sat at the kitchen table looking outside as half-dollar-sized snowflakes fell like feathers in the moonlight.

"Doesn't get better than this," Frank said with a sigh after finishing his last bite. Kate smiled, replying,

"I thought you hated the snow."

"I like it from here!"

"Yeah, it's pretty special." Frank moved his foot to hers and smiled as their feet touched. Kate rolled her free foot toward his. As it slid across the floor, it found the microscopic KSP element missed by the broom earlier. Just then, there were thirty blinding white flashes. For Kate and Frank, all time was stretched, the room turned pure white, the noise of the wood crackling in the woodstove was amplified, and the last bite of food in their mouths became a symphony of flavor. Their lives were instantly changed, and an unbelievable adventure began.

About The Author

Erik R. Eide was born in the Chicago area. California's coast became his habitat before Seattle came to be a second hometown. He currently lives in Dallas/Fort Worth, Texas. His passions include faith, family, writing, music production and meatloaf.
eideologically.com
erik@eideological.com

More Books by Erik R. Eide

The Landfill Collective

Book One-"The Landfill" is a fast-paced science fiction adventure through time, galaxies, and societies. A book, glazed like a lemon filled donut with the bizarre to the profound. Thick layers of chocolate excitement for your brain, and heavy meatloaf-like concepts for your heart. There's love and great evil within this strange tale, exploring mind, body, spirit. Come along for the ride and bring your own cup of coffee! From the text-"On the way down, the box was saturated with a new experimental genetic pretreatment, designed to humanely destroy the sentient nature of non-animal biology. Unfortunately, mixed with the decontamination/deodorizing chemical aerosol used in this morning's bulkhead failure, this genetic treatment yielded shocking results. Some forces within the landfill should never have been awakened yet, in the hour of their greatest need, help will come from the same area of the ship."

The Hydra
Book Two-"The Hydra" continues the parable of struggles between forces of light and darkness. The Collective, controlling an army of host bodies, liberates a convicted traitor in order to mastermind the ultimate weapon of terror. The "Shǒuhù Zhě" (Keepers of Honor, the elite warriors of Jook-sing) join with freedom fighters of many worlds to war against an enemy using a quantum-based weapon of mass destruction. The Hydra combines absurd comedy, off-centered ideas, and ties them with concepts relative to our world. It's an escape from orthodox science fiction, exploring faith, time travel, new worlds, and old. A book deliciously baked together like a well-

seasoned meatloaf. Come along for the ride and bring your cup of coffee. Donuts will be provided.